GUN FOR REVENGE

While Gabriel Moonlight hides out in Mexico, Ellen Kincaide asks him to avenge the death of her sister and Gabriel's former girlfriend, Cally. He refuses, but when Ellen is kidnapped by bandits Gabriel sets out to rescue her. Then he has a change of heart and promises to kill the man who murdered Cally. But he discovers the identity of the murderer and knows that to exact retribution means almost certain death. Even so, a promise is a promise.

STEVE HAYES

GUN FOR REVENGE

Complete and Unabridged

LINFORD
Leicester

First published in Great Britain in 2008 by
Robert Hale Limited
London

First Linford Edition
published 2009
by arrangement with
Robert Hale Limited
London

British Library CIP Data

Hayes, Steve.
  Guns for revenge. - - (Linford western library)
  1. Western stories.
  2. Large type books.
  I. Title II. Series
  823.9′2–dc22

ISBN 978–1–84782–925–2

Published by
F. A. Thorpe (Publishing)
Anstey, Leicestershire

Set by Words & Graphics Ltd.
Anstey, Leicestershire
Printed and bound in Great Britain by
T. J. International Ltd., Padstow, Cornwall

This book is printed on acid-free paper

This is for my wife, Robbin
and
Louis L'Amour
Thanks for your friendship

Prologue

He was almost out of the Sierra Madre now. Another grueling day's descent, two at most, he thought, and he would reach the foothills. Hopefully, there or in the adjoining valley he'd glimpsed from the ridgeline, he could find a remote area where he could build some kind of shelter and hole up for a spell.

Gunshots interrupted his thinking. Reining up, the tall man sat motionless in the saddle, listening intently as he tried to pinpoint exactly where the shots had come from. It wasn't easy. The shots, made by rifles and pistols, were being fired so rapidly they sounded more like fireworks exploding than gunfire. He listened as their echoes bounced off the steep, brush-covered hills surrounding him — and finally decided they were coming from a wooded canyon to his right.

1

He pulled his Winchester from its boot and nudged the all-black stallion forward, ready to shoot anyone he saw who appeared threatening.

Ahead, the winding dirt trail descended through dense, waist-high brush and clumps of cactus and stumpy pine trees. Here and there great slabs of rock bared themselves, his keen gaze spotting tiny mottled-green lizards basking in the glaring, oven-hot sun.

As he approached a fork in the trail, the shots stopped as suddenly as they began. Again, he reined up. Now he could hear raucous laughter and drunken voices — men, whooping it up, he decided. Probably bandidos celebrating the spoils from their last raid. Wanting no trouble, he guided the horse toward the fork that led away from the canyon.

That was when he heard the scream — a man's scream, one long wailing cry filled with despair and excruciating agony.

He hesitated. He hated to think of what kind of torture was needed to

2

produce a scream that awful, but at the same time he remembered why he had come to Mexico in the first place; deciding this was none of his business, he urged the stallion forward.

A second scream, just as agonizing to his ear as the first, made him rein up again. Damn, the tall man thought. Damn, damn, damn. And against his better judgment he turned the horse around and headed it toward the screams.

He dismounted at the mouth of the canyon, chambered a shell into his Winchester and crawled through the brush toward a clearing from which smoke spiraled up. The screams had stopped, but he could now hear the men taunting their victim. Though they spoke in Spanish he understood every word and realized they were demanding that their prisoner reveal the where-abouts of his gold — gold they apparently believed he'd cached some-where.

Eventually he parted the brush

fringing the clearing and saw six rag-
gedly dressed bandits gathered around
an old, white-bearded prospector who
was spread-eagled over a fire. Barely
alive, his clothes had been burned off
and his flesh charred by the flames.

Enraged, the tall man got to his feet,
steadied himself and shot the nearest
bandit, who collapsed, dead. He killed
two more before the others had time to
grab their rifles. Then, grimly walking
toward them, he pumped shot after
shot into the three remaining bandidos
until all of them lay dead.

Two of them fell into the fire, their
filthy rags promptly ignited by the
flames. Ignoring them, the tall man
dropped his Winchester, gently picked
up the old prospector and carried him
to the rocks where he made him as
comfortable as possible.

There was nothing anyone could do
for him. The tall man pressed his ear
against the old-timer's lips and heard
his last words:

'M-Miss Alice,' he whispered, ' — is

sh-she still 'live?'

The tall man looked around. There were no other human beings in sight, but a few yards away a pack-mule lay dead on its side. He shook his head. The prospector, his facial skin so charred by the flames that the cheek bones showed, blinked his thanks.

'G-Gold,' he said, his burned lips barely moving. 'B-Buried it . . . 'neath . . . rocks by c-cabin . . . west end . . . valley b-below . . . '

The tall man nodded to show he understood.

'N-Not much . . . but . . . 'nuff for a grub s-stake . . . '

'Thanks,' the tall man said. 'But I ain't a prospector.'

The dying man frowned, puzzled. 'Why . . . y-you here . . . then?'

Before the tall man could reply, the prospector's eyes rolled upward and he stiffened. The tall man didn't need to check his pulse to know the old-timer was dead. Gently, he closed the prospector's blackened eyelids.

Overhead, buzzards were already circling.

The tall man decided to cheat them of at least one meal. He covered the prospector's corpse with rocks, then stepped into the saddle and rode away from the canyon.

1

The stallion saw the wagon first. Though it was just entering the valley and still a mile off, the smell of strangers made the horse nervous. It snorted, tossing its head so that its long black mane gleamed in the afternoon sunlight, and anxiously pawed the ground. Then, after cantering up the steep rise to the cabin, it stopped beside a man dozing on the doorstep and whinnied.

'It's OK,' the man said softly. 'I see 'em.'

He rose and he looked around to make sure no other strangers were on the horizon and then entered the cabin. He was a tall, rangy man who moved with the lethal ease of an Apache. His long once-black hair was now prematurely flecked with gray and his eyes, deep-set and the palest of blues, had a wintry chill to them that made most men step aside rather than risk a fight. He grabbed a well-oiled Winchester '73 and field glasses from the deer rack above the door and returned outside.

The wagon inched across the flat scrubland toward him, its image distorted by heat waves rising from the sun-baked desert. The man held the glasses to his eyes, adjusting the focus until suddenly the mule-drawn wagon leaped into view.

Raising the glasses a fraction, he focused on the two people riding on it. The driver was an old Mexican whose weathered brown face was barely visible below the brim of his frayed sombrero, while the passenger was a woman dressed all in black, as if in mourning. Despite the broiling sun, she wore Sunday-morning gloves and kept her hands clasped primly in her lap. A dust-caked veil prevented him from seeing what she looked like, but by her stylish hat the man guessed she was American.

No threat there, he thought. The Mex is too old to be a *pistolero* and the woman so slender I could break her like a stick. But she's iron-willed, he thought admiringly, to sit so ladylike on a buckboard in this God-awful heat.

He lowered the glasses and returned to the doorstep. On the way he brushed past the stallion. He came too close to suit the all-black Morgan. It took a nip at him, then shied away before the man could slap it with his old, sweat-stained campaign hat.

Once seated, the man hung the glasses around his neck, rested the rifle across his knees and pulled his hat down so that most of his face was hidden by the brim. He then leaned back against the door, head tilted up so he could watch the wagon approaching.

He waited, with a patience only a man who has served time behind bars could possess, and after what seemed like an eternity the wagon at last reined up in front of him.

'*Buenos tardes, señor,*' the old

Mexican said politely.

'*Buenos tardes.*' The man rose, tipped his hat to the woman and then pointed his rifle toward the stream that descended from the Sierra Madre foothills and ran curving between the rocks behind the cabin. 'You're welcome to water the mules if you've a mind to.'

'*Mucho gracias, señor.*'

'An' if you're hungry, there's coffee an' biscuits left over from a batch I made this mornin'.'

The woman, who had been studying him from behind her veil, now leaned forward wearily as if to get a closer look.

'That's most generous of you,' she said in a parched, cultured voice. 'But first I'd like to introduce myself and my companion. I'm Miss Kincaide, Ellen Kincaide, and this is my good friend, Señor Miguel Escalero.'

She waited, expecting the man to respond by telling her his name. When he didn't, she steadied herself by grasping the side of the wagon and said:

'And you are, *señor?*'

He didn't answer. But instinctively, his finger curled around the rifle trigger.

'Forgive me,' she said, alarmed. 'I'm not trying to be nosy. I'm only asking because I'm looking for someone.'

He eyed her suspiciously, wishing now he hadn't been so sociable.

'An' who might that be?'

'A man . . . about your age . . . who once knew my sister in Santa Rosa.'

Santa Rosa! The name of the New Mexico pueblo leaped out of his past.

Intrigued, he stepped closer to the woman. 'Be obliged if you'd lift your veil, ma'am.'

Ellen Kincaide obeyed, her stiff, aching muscles crying out for rest.

The man frowned, surprised. She was younger than he had expected by the mature timbre of her voice: in her late twenties, at most. Even more surprising, her pale, fine-boned oval face, though caked with trail dust that

11

had been kicked up by the mules and had seeped through her veil, looked vaguely familiar; especially her expressive, wide-set violet eyes and elegantly tilted chin.

'Do I know you, ma'am?'

'I don't believe so. This is my first venture into Mexico. And I was away at school when the man I'm looking for was in Santa Rosa. But Cally said he came into her cantina every night — '

'Cally?' Once more his past came rushing back to him, along with a flood of buried emotions that he had forgotten existed. 'Your sister's name is Cally?'

'Yes. Cally Sage. She kept her husband's name after he suddenly died of pneumonia.'

Gabriel smiled inwardly. Willard Sage, a railroad gambler with ten-cent morals and hundred-dollar dreams, had died of lead poisoning when a passenger caught him dealing from the bottom of the deck.

'You *did* know her, didn't you?' Ellen

persisted. 'I can tell by the way you just looked.'

'It's possible,' he said guardedly. 'I've 'chased the rabbit' in a cantina or two.'

'Then for heaven's sake tell me your name! Because if you are the man I pray you are then this god-forsaken journey is finally over.'

He hesitated, still surprised to find himself talking to Cally's sister after all these years, then said quietly:

'It's Moonlight, ma'am. Gabriel Moonlight.'

For a moment he thought she was going to faint from disappointment. The old Mexican thought the same thing and quickly grabbed her arms, steadying her.

'It — it's all right, I'm fine,' Ellen assured him. Pulling herself together, she turned to Gabriel. 'Thank you, Mr Moonlight. I'm sorry if I made you suspicious, but — '

'So I ain't the man you're lookin' for?'

'No. His name's Mesquite Jennings.'

Expecting as much, Gabriel forced himself not to react.

'An' this Jennings fella — it's important you find him?'

'A matter of life and death.'

She bravely fought back tears, looking so distressed he was tempted to tell her the truth. But before he could decide if she was worth risking his life for, she gathered herself and asked him if the coffee and biscuits he had offered were still available.

'Take but a minute to heat up, ma'am.'

'Then I accept. Now if you'll kindly help me down, I'll — ' She broke off, eyes rolling up into her head, and collapsed into his outstretched arms.

2

Gabriel carried the still-unconscious woman into the cabin, put her on his cot and slipped a pillow under her head. Then, after dipping a towel in the bucket of water he kept by the stove, he bathed her grimy face and parched lips and placed the cool wet cloth on her forehead.

'How long you been eatin' dust?' he asked Escalero.

'Six — maybe eight days, I think, señor.'

'From where?'

'North of the border, señor. Las Cruces.' Sombrero in hand, he looked at the woman he'd befriended two years ago with admiration. 'It is the miracle of miracles that Sis — the señorita did not collapse long before this.'

Gabriel had wondered the same thing about the old man but, after a second look at him, changed his mind. Though small, and at least seventy, he looked tough as goat meat. Yet there was an air of dignity about him. Below his large, drooping white mustache his mouth had an honest set to it; and under bristly white eyebrows his brown eyes were bright with compassion.

Taking a half-full bottle of J. H. Cutter from a cupboard, Gabriel removed the cork and wiped the only glass he owned clean on his sleeve before pouring some whiskey into it. He then gently pried open Ellen's lips and dribbled a few drops into her mouth.

She choked, coughing and sputtering as the alcohol burned her throat, and stared vacantly about her.

'Easy, lady,' he said quietly. 'Take it slow.'

It took a few minutes but eventually Ellen recovered enough to sit up. Gabriel filled a tin basin from the water barrel out back and set it on the table so she could wash the trail dirt from her face and hands.

Having not seen a white woman since he'd fled across the border almost two years ago, he watched her out the corner of his eye as he stoked the embers and heated the coffee and biscuits atop the stove. Eggshells lay scattered around the old greasy skillet. He hadn't noticed them at breakfast, or if he had they hadn't bothered him, but now because of the woman they did and he scraped them up with the spatula and dumped them into the flames. If she was still here tomorrow, he told himself, he must be more careful when he cracked his eggs into the spitting bacon grease.

Why it would bother him if Cally's sister thought he was messy, he couldn't explain. But it did and he accepted it with the same stoic resignation he accepted the stallion's sour disposition or the mud that every year threatened to flood his cabin during rainy season.

As he continued to watch her something puzzled him; earlier, when she had prepared to wash, she'd rolled up her sleeves and opened her blouse at her throat, but never removed her hat. He wondered why. Years ago he'd worked as a hostler at a stagecoach stop and the first thing women did when they came inside to clean up was take off their hats.

He also noticed that the upper part of her forehead was much paler than the rest of her face, as if it hadn't seen the sun in a long time. He wondered what had made the mark. But feeling it would be impertinent to ask her, he pushed it from his mind. He brought the now-hot coffee and biscuits to the table and stood there, silently leaning against the door, while she ate and drank.

'Aren't you going to join me?'

'I already ate, ma'am.'

'Some coffee, then?'

Rather than tell her he only had one cup, he said: 'Thanks. I've had my fill.'

Ellen continued eating for a few moments before saying: 'These biscuits are . . . well, they're wonderful. So soft and flaky. Far better than any I've ever made.'

He accepted her compliment in silence.

'You . . . uh . . . live here by yourself, Mr Moonlight?'

He nodded.

'Don't you ever get lonely?'

He shook his head.

'How extraordinary. I would never have thought that by looking at you.'

Curiosity aroused, he said: 'What would you have thought?'

'Well, of course I don't know you but . . . you give me the impression that you haven't always been a loner — that once you were full of fun and liked having a good time.'

'You can tell all that just by lookin' at me?'

She sensed he resented her prying, though she couldn't imagine why, and shrugged. 'Call it woman's intuition.'

She waited for him to confirm or deny her impression of him, but he remained silent.

'Personally, I enjoy having people around me. The more the merrier — which I'm afraid often conflicts with my . . . uh . . . vocation.' She noticed Escalero signaling to her with his eyes. As if reminded of something, she fell silent and finished her coffee. Its harsh bitterness, made worse by reheating, made her grimace. But she drank it without complaint, all the while watched over by the old Mexican.

His protectiveness of her was endearing; though equally parched and hungry, he refused to drink or eat until she assured him that she was all right. He then gulped down a full dipper of water, humbly accepted two of the remaining biscuits and went outside.

Gabriel watched him through the window. He expected Escalero to find some shade and eat; instead the old man wearily unhitched the mules from the wagon and led them down to the stream. There, while they drank, he removed his *huaraches*, dipped his bare feet into the water, closed his eyes and rocked with contentment. Then, and only then, did he start eating the biscuits.

'That old Mex you're travelin' with, he's got grit.'

Ellen Kincaide nodded. 'I never would've made it here without Miguel. He's been my guardian angel.'

'You needed one, if you don't mind me sayin'.'

'Really? Why's that?'

'The Sierras, ma'am. They're a-crawl with *bandidos*, all just itchin' to rob folks like you. It's nigh on a miracle you made it through alive.'

'If it is, it's a wasted one.' She yawned wearily. 'After talking to the *Rurales* in San Dimas, I was certain you were the man I was looking for.'

Gabriel felt the hair prickling on the back of his neck.

'You talked to the *Rurales* about me?'

'Yes. Well, no, not about you. About Mesquite Jennings. To Captain Morales, I believe his name was.'

'Mind tellin' me what you said?'

She yawned again, politely trying to conceal it behind her hand.

'I don't recall my exact words, but basically I told him I was trying to find an American named Mesquite Jennings — '

'What'd he say?'

'That he didn't know any men by that name — actually he used the word gringo, which I found offensive — and asked me if I knew what he looked like.' She paused and yawned behind her hand again. 'I described Jennings the way Cally told me he looked — tall, lean, lots of dark hair and very light blue eyes — and Captain Morales immediately suggested you might be the man I'm looking for.'

'That description fits a lot of men besides me.'

'I know. But how many of them are holed up near San Dimas?'

'Cally tell you that, too?'

'Yes — in strict confidence, of course.'

'So you didn't mention it to Captain Morales?'

'No — '

'Or let it drop that Jennings was a gunfighter with a rope waitin' for him across the border?'

'My God, no! Give me credit for some brains, Mr Moonlight.'

He realized he'd pushed her too far.

'Sorry . . . I meant no offense.'

'I'm not offended. I'm just surprised.'

' 'Bout what?'

'That since you're not Mesquite Jennings, you'd be upset that I might have given Captain Morales the impression he's a wanted man.'

Feeling he was being baited, Gabriel kept silent.

'Is he a friend of yours, by chance?'

He shook his head.

'Do you happen to know where he is?'

'Nope.'

She studied him, thinking he had the palest blue eyes she'd ever seen. She also detected a trace of uneasiness in them, prompting her to say:

'I don't mean to suggest you're a liar, Mr Moonlight, but are you positive you're not Mesquite Jennings? I've ridden an awful long way and God only knows where I'll look next.'

'Maybe it's time you stopped lookin',' he said. 'Gave up this wild-goose chase an' went back to Las Cruces.'

'Never,' Ellen replied. 'I've sacrificed too much to turn back now.' Fighting to stay awake, she took another sip of coffee.

Gabriel scuffed the toe of his boot on the floor, a nervous habit he betrayed unconsciously.

'It's none of my business, I know, but what's so all-fired important about Jennings that makes you willin' to risk your life?'

'I'm afraid that's personal,' she said. She yawned again, too tired now to cover her mouth. Her eyelids drooped. She struggled to keep them open, but it was a losing battle. And within moments, her head fell forward and she drifted off.

Gabriel studied her, trying to decide what to do next. He was tempted to wake her up and send her and the old Mexican on their way. But she looked so exhausted he couldn't bring himself to do it. Besides, she was the sister of a woman he'd once loved and for that reason, if no other, she deserved to be treated kindly.

So, against his better judgment, he carried her to his cot, gently laid her down and covered her with a blanket. In the process her hat came off. He set it on the table, careful not to crease the brim or snag the dust-caked veil. Then he pulled the chair up beside her, fired a match, lit a cigar and smoked while she slept.

As he sat there idling puffing out smoke rings, he studied the young woman more closely. Without her hat, the first thing that jumped out at him was her hair — or lack of it. The color of winter honey, it was closely cropped all over her head. Almost, he thought, as if it had once been shaved and was now growing back.

He'd never seen such an odd, unattractive hairstyle on a woman. He wondered what could have possibly induced her to cut all her hair off. He had never known a man who wasn't attracted to long hair on a woman or a woman who didn't use her seductive tresses to her advantage. Yet this one seemed too cultured, too intelligent to have deliberately shorn her locks without good reason. He racked his brains and finally decided that she must have thought there were still Apaches lurking in the Sierra Madres and hoped that her hairless scalp wouldn't appeal to them.

He also noticed that without dust and sweat caking her face, she was prettier than he'd first realized. No, she was more than pretty, he thought. There was something else about her that until now he had missed, something that transcended any physical beauty. He studied her carefully, wondering what it was. For a while nothing came to him. But after he'd smoked his cigar down to the ash, it hit him at last: there was an aura of pureness about her, a shining innocence that radiated from her face — even in sleep.

His thoughts were interrupted by the stallion's sharp whinny. Almost at once came the sound of horses. Gabriel rose, looked out the window and saw three riders approaching from the direction of San Dimas.

They were large men, armed with rifles and tied-down six-guns, their grimy hats pulled low over their bearded faces.

Border trash, Gabriel thought disgustedly. Maybe even bounty hunters. Either way, they were unwelcome. He grabbed his Winchester and went outside to meet them.

3

The three riders reined up in front of Gabriel but made no attempt to dismount. The eldest, a slump-shouldered, gray-haired gringo of about fifty wearing a patch over one eye, spat tobacco juice at a nearby chicken. He hit it squarely on the head, sending it clucking into the barn. He then grinned, showing a mouthful of broken brown teeth, and tipped his hat at Gabriel.

'Afternoon to ya, mister . . . '

Gabriel nodded but said nothing. His keen gaze noticed bulges under the shirts of all three men, indicating they were carrying belly-guns.

'My boys'n me, we was wonderin' if you might spare some water for our horses?'

'Help yourselves.'

'Some of that coffee I smell would be welcome, too,' said the youngest of the

28

three. His red mustache and the bearded corners of his mouth were stained yellow with snuff and Gabriel could smell him from where he stood.

'Sorry. Coffee's all used up.'

'Biscuits too, I bet?' said the other man. He was the smallest of the three but there was a rabid meanness to his squinted eyes that told Gabriel to shoot him first.

'Down to the last crumb,' he said mildly.

Their smiles hardened and their hands inched toward their belly guns. For a moment Gabriel thought they might make their play. But then the older man grinned, easing the tension.

'Seems like that's the way our luck's been runnin' lately,' he said and nudged his horse downhill toward the stream.

As they descended the slope all of them looked long and hard at the stallion grazing nearby. Their presence disturbed the Morgan, and with an angry flick of its tail it moved away and didn't stop until it was safely out of reach of their lariats.

From where he sat by the stream Escalero had been watching the riders since their arrival. As they drew close, his right hand slipped inside his loose shirt and gripped the pistol hidden there.

But the riders ignored him. Dismounting, they turned their horses loose to drink and flopped down beside the stream. Immersing their faces in the water, they drank greedily, then straightened up and shook themselves like stray mongrels.

Gabriel leaned against the side of the cabin and watched them. Other than Ellen and Escalero he hadn't seen a human being in over two months. To have these misfits appear right on their heels and from the same direction spelled trouble. San Dimas was close enough to the border to attract outlaws and riff-raff from both countries. These weasels may have even overheard Ellen telling someone that she was looking for Mesquite Jennings and followed her from New Mexico, in which case they were definitely bounty hunters.

Gabriel wondered if he should awaken her and warn her to stay in the cabin until after the men left. But there wasn't time. Already the three of them were riding up the slope toward him.

Gabriel kept his finger on the rifle trigger, ready to burn powder at any hint of trouble. But either he was mistaken about the riders' intentions or they weren't ready to test him. Because after cresting the rise, they waved their thanks and rode off without stopping.

He watched them disappear into the distant heat waves and felt a sense of relief. Of course, he thought, they could be trying to fool him; intending to double back later and pick up their 'dead or alive' reward, but —

His thoughts were interrupted by a sound behind him. Turning, he saw Ellen watching him from the doorway.

'Must be your day for visitors, Mr Moonlight.'

'Must be,' he said grimly. He brushed

past her into the cabin and returned the Winchester to its antler cradle.

Troubled, Ellen joined him.

'Am I responsible for those men showing up here?'

He shrugged his broad, hard-muscled shoulders.

'Is that a yes or a no?'

'Not every question has a simple answer, ma'am.'

'In other words, you don't know?'

He didn't answer. She could tell he didn't like being pressed, but was too stubborn to back down.

'You think I'm pushy, don't you?'

Truthfully, he wasn't sure what he thought. He liked her directness but hated being backed against a wall.

He said quietly: 'When you were passin' through San Dimas did you happen to see those three men — talk to them, maybe?'

'Heavens, no.'

'How 'bout the old man?'

'Impossible. He never left my side.'

Gabriel shrugged, as if to say she had

answered her own question.

Ellen felt relieved. She also found herself surprised that she cared whether he blamed her not. After all, she thought, what could he possibly mean to her? In a few hours she and Miguel would be on their way, and she would never see him again. Yet, she had to admit there was something appealing about him; appealing and at the same time quite deadly. And not just because of his uncanny light-blue eyes.

Now, watching him straighten the blanket on his cot, she remembered that earlier she had fallen asleep at the table.

'I never thanked you for letting me use your bed.'

He shrugged indifferently. 'I figured you'd be a sight more comfortable there.'

'That was most thoughtful of you. As you can guess, I haven't slept much lately. In fact, hardly at all since we left Las Cruces.' She smiled, embarrassed. 'I'm sure that sounds silly to you. You probably sleep just as well on the trail as . . . ' She caught him looking at her hair and self-consciously ran her fingers through the wispy mat of curls.

'You're wondering why, aren't you?'

'Thought did cross my mind, yes, ma'am. On account of Apaches, maybe?'

'Apaches?'

He could see she had no idea what he was talking about and feeling foolish, said: 'No matter. Thirsty, are you?'

'Enough to drink that whole stream out there.'

She was so refreshingly honest he wasn't sure how to deal with her. For months at a time his only outlet for conversation was the stallion. And the ill-tempered horse, like Gabriel, preferred silence.

'I'm also famished. I know that's not very ladylike. Ladies are required to be refined and to nibble daintily at their food. But to be perfectly honest, Mr Moonlight, after all I've been through recently I don't feel very dainty or ladylike.'

She waited for him to reply. When he didn't, she said: 'You're not very talkative, are you?'

He didn't answer, feeling silence was the best way to answer her question.

'Perhaps I should respect that and not talk so much myself.'

'That ain't necessary. I got no quarrel with talkin'. It's just . . . ' He toed the floor awkwardly. 'I'm not used to it on account of I don't get much company.'

Ellen looked around, suddenly noticing the scarcity of furniture: all handmade, there was only one chair, a table, cot, clothes-chest and a standing cupboard that doubled as a pantry.

'I never would have guessed that,' she said impishly.

Gabriel smiled. He liked a woman with humor.

Outside, the stallion whinnied angrily. Gabriel glanced out the window, hoping the Morgan wasn't trying to bite the old Mexican.

'That's a magnificent horse you have, Mr Moonlight.'

'Gabe,' he said.

'I beg your pardon?'

'Nobody calls me Moonlight or Gabriel. Just Gabe.'

'Oh . . . '

'Not that I'm ashamed of my name or anythin'. But when your surname's as fancy as Moonlight, attachin' a tag like Gabriel to it is like addin' insult to injury.'

'I suppose . . . '

'You don't agree?'

'Well, Gabriel is very Biblical.'

'Biblical don't hold much salt in a cantina.'

'Gabriel was supposed to be God's messenger.'

'Try tellin' that to a fella who's pie-eyed. Only message he's got is a fist to your face.'

'Really?' She hadn't thought of it that way. 'Well, your face doesn't look like it's known too many fists.' She paused, suddenly embarrassed by her forwardness, then said: 'Very well. Gabe it is. But if we're going to be on a first-name basis, I insist you call me Ellen or Ellie, whichever you prefer.'

'Ellie,' he said without hesitation. 'It rolls easier off the tongue.'

They lapsed into a silence that became awkward.

'It's a Morgan,' Gabriel added, not wanting the conversation to die. 'My horse, I mean.'

'Yes, I know. You can always tell by the proud arch of their necks and how compact and muscular the body is. Goes fourteen and a half hands, I'd say.'

He realized his mouth was open and quickly closed it.

'Don't look so surprised,' she laughed. 'Just because I'm a woman doesn't mean I can't know about horses.'

'I didn't mean to imply — '

'I learned about Morgans from my Grampa Tate. For years he made a living rounding up broomtails and selling them to the Army. But in '89, when wild horses got scarce, he started a riding stable for the Las Cruces gentry. All his horses are fine animals but his favorites are two Morgans, Duke and King. He treats them like sons. Says other than Arabs, Morgans are the finest horses alive.'

And the goddamn meanest, Gabriel thought.

'They're all supposed to be descended from one stallion: Justice Morgan, wasn't it?'

'Justin.'

'Ah. And how did you come by such a fine animal?'

'Well, I didn't steal him,' he said bluntly.

'That thought never occurred to me, Mr Moonlight.'

'Gabe.'

Now it was her turn to be silent.

'I won Brandy in a poker game. Aces an' eights. Dead man's hand. Unlucky for Hickok, lucky for me.'

The idea of gambling didn't seem to please her.

'If you're still hungry, I got a mess of stew I could heat up,' he offered. 'An' there's smoked venison hangin' in the pantry. Or I could fry you up some eggs an' ham — '

'Stew sounds perfect,' Ellen said. She stood up, swayed on wobbly legs and would have fallen if he hadn't caught her.

'Careful, ma'am.' He helped her walk to the table and gently lowered her into the chair.

'Thank you, Mr — Gabe. I'm afraid I'm not as strong as I thought. By the way,' she said looking around, 'where's Miguel?'

'At the creek, waterin' the mules.'

'Oh. Yes, of course, the mules. Poor things. The drive was very hard on them. We ran out of water a day's ride from San Dimas and all the natural water holes Miguel had counted on were either dried up or poisoned by alkali, and undrinkable.' She yawned and stretched the stiffness from her muscles. 'Can you believe it, I'm still worn out.'

'The old man said you've been

movin' steady for over a week.'

'Yes, though it felt more like a month.' She gingerly shifted positions on the chair, wincing as her blisters chafed. 'I never realized a wagon could be so bumpy or a seat so hard.'

Gabriel busied himself at the stove. After raking the embers with a poker he clattered pots and pans around, making room over the heat for a heavy blackened kettle of stew.

Too tired to offer to help, Ellen watched him stirring the stew. Occasionally he tasted it on a wooden ladle, adding either a pinch of salt, pepper or herbs, and once he thickened it with a handful of flour. His skill as a cook impressed and surprised her. It made her realize he was a strange mix of a man. He had the rugged, lean body of a range rider and his Levis and denim shirt were worn and faded from endless hours in the saddle, yet his familiarity with cooking suggested he'd been living alone for a long time.

Though his back was to the woman,

Gabriel could feel her stare. He felt obliged to say: 'Won't be too long now. An' if you've a mind, I still got two biscuits left.'

'Gabe,' she said sleepily, 'you're nothing short of a Godsend.' Yawning, she rested her cheek on her folded arms and drifted off to sleep.

4

It was almost dawn when Ellen next awoke. Overtired, she had slept like the dead, barely moving from the position in which Gabriel had placed her after carrying her — for the second time — from the table.

She sat up, rubbed the sleep from her eyes and gazed about her. Nearby, Gabriel sat dozing under a blanket. She smiled, grateful for his kind support. Behind him, she saw Escalero curled up by the stove. Her heart warmed at the sight of the old man. Dear Miguel, she thought lovingly. Where would she be without him? Crossing herself, she thanked God for protecting the three of them through the night.

She would have continued praying, but her stirring had aroused Gabriel. He came instantly awake, the blanket sliding off his lap revealing a .44–40

Remington long-barrel revolver clasped in his hand.

'My goodness, are you expecting trouble?'

'Never hurts to be prepared.'

'No . . . I suppose not.' She watched him stuff the big bluish six-gun into his old Levis before adding: 'Those three men — you think they might return?'

'I doubt it,' Gabriel said, not wanting to alarm her.

'Earlier, you mentioned Apaches. Are there still raiding parties down here?'

'No. Apaches all went north in '86 when Geronimo surrendered. Might be some Yaquis or Pimas crossed over from Arizona. Maybe even a few Maricopas. But they're all mostly sociable.'

'Then why the pistol?'

'Ain't a pistol,' Gabriel said, stalling. 'It's a revolver.'

'Well, whatever it is, why are you holding it as if you're ready to shoot someone?'

'Bears,' he said, grabbing the first lie that came to mind. 'Sometimes they get to nosin' around, catch wind of honey or fresh-killed meat and then break in. Always best to be prepared.'

'Oh-h . . . yes, of course. Bears. Odd. I hadn't counted on bears.'

'It's the things you don't count on, ma'am, likely to kill you the quickest.'

'Ellie, remember? We made a deal.'

Just then a faint noise made Gabriel whirl around, the revolver seeming to leap into his hand. When he saw it was Escalero getting to his feet he relaxed, gently lowered the hammer and saluted the old man with the Remington.

Escalero, knowing he'd just faced death, humbly bowed his head and apologized for startling Gabriel.

'He thought you were a bear,' laughed Ellen. 'Says they break in from time to time and steal his honey.'

Escalero gave Gabriel a knowing look, just to let him know that he knew there were no bears around, but said nothing.

Gabriel stamped his feet to get the blood going. 'I better go rustle up some eggs,' he said. The door slammed behind him.

Ellen looked out the window and saw him entering the barn. Moments later several chickens flew out, squawking.

It reminded her of her childhood after her parents died. Every day, just before dawn, she would leave Cally asleep in the bed beside her and sneak into their grandfather's barn to watch the chickens laying eggs. Occasionally, she cupped one in her hands. There was something so perfect about a warm, just-laid egg that she regretted having to take them from the hens, knowing that shortly they would be cracked open and their gooey innards spread sizzling in a frying pan.

Her memories made her smile. She felt strangely at home here and wondered why. No place could be more desolate or hostile. And no man could be more different from the young gentlemen she was familiar with in Las Cruces. His reclusive manner, reluctance to talk and the deadly speed with which he drew his gun — all suggested that he was hiding out here, was perhaps a fugitive or even the gun-fighter, Mesquite Jenkins. Yet, strangely, she felt no fear when she was with him. On the contrary, she'd never felt safer.

Outside, the stallion suddenly neighed and came charging into view. At first she thought the Morgan was just pranc-ing around, enjoying its freedom; but when it lowered its head and lunged at something, teeth snapping, she realized it was chasing a fleeing rooster. Amused, she turned and looked at Escalero.

The old Mexican seemed to know what she was going to say, and quickly looked away.

'Now Miguel, don't try to ignore me.'

He met her gaze and held it.

'Forgive me, Sister.'

'I asked you not to call me that, remember?' Then as he nodded his apology: 'I know you don't agree with what I'm doing. And I respect you for that. It's your right. But at least tell me what you think of Señor Moonlight?'

'I do not think of him at all, Sister.'

'Nonsense. I saw you watching him. Like you watch all men I come in contact with.'

'Forgive me, Sister. I will not do it again.'

'I'm not scolding you, Miguel. I'm just curious to know what you think of him.'

The old man stalled, twisting the frayed brim of his sombrero between his leathery fingers.

'Well?' she demanded. 'The truth now.'

'He is a man I would trust your life with, Sister.'

Ellen smiled. It was exactly the answer she wanted to hear.

5

After breakfast, Ellen felt strong enough to take a walk. Escalero got up from a shady spot beside the cabin, intending to join her. But she gestured for him to stay where he was and started down the slope to the stream.

Though just a few minutes past eight, it was already hot and the air so dry it made her trail-raw eyes feel like there was grit in them. Kneeling on a flat rock beside the stream, she splashed water on her face. Its coolness soothed her burning eyes but stung her chapped lips.

Suddenly, soundlessly, he was standing beside her, holding her hat.

'Better put this on, ma'am, 'fore you get sunburned.'

She placed the hat on her head, asking: 'Are you ever going to call me Ellie?'

'You ever gonna tell me why you shaved your head?'

She laughed. 'Why, Gabriel Moonlight, you're as pushy as I am.'

'Wasn't my intention.' He turned to leave.

'Wait. I'll tell you . . . ' Ellen ran her fingers through her wispy buttery curls and thought a moment before saying: 'It's growing out now . . . '

He kept silent, hoping she'd continue.

'Many of the sisters at the convent do it. I didn't want to. In fact I hated the idea, but . . . ' She shrugged and self-consciously touched her hair. 'You may not believe me, Gabe, but I had very pretty hair. It hung halfway down my back. I used to get lots of compliments on it and at night, just before going to bed, I always brushed it one hundred times so it would shine. But long hair gets hot and sweaty under a coronet — '

'A what?'

'Coronet. That's a nun's hat. These

days, coronets are considered somewhat medieval and a lot of sisters in other convents wear much smaller hats. But our order insists we wear one — along with an under-cap that covers our forehead in front.'

Realizing now why the upper half of her forehead was so pale, he said: 'So that's what the old man meant — '

'Miguel told you I was a nun?'

'No, but he started to call you 'Sister' once an' then corrected himself.'

'Poor sweet man. I can't blame him. It's been awfully difficult for him. He's worked at the convent for most of his life, and been a close part of mine for almost two years. And then out of the blue I quit the order and ask him to come with me to — '

'You're not a nun any more?'

'I never actually was one. Not officially. I was a novice. I still had a few months left before I completed my novitiate. That's a training period,' she explained, seeing he didn't understand the word. 'Sort of like, well, like probation. All novices are required to go through it in order to prove they are suitably 'called' to the religious life.'

He toed the dirt with his boot and tugged at his thick, graying dark hair.

'An' you, you didn't figure you were 'called'?'

'At first I did. I was absolutely committed. But after a few months I felt isolated and wasn't so sure. Neither was Mother Superior. We had several long talks about it. I tried to be honest with her, to tell her how I really felt, how I missed being around lots of people, having fun and dancing and playing the harpsichord and, well, that concerned her. She reminded me that giving myself over to God and spreading his word was a full-time, lifelong commitment. I knew she was right and that I was just being weak and tempted by material pleasures . . . but I still couldn't decide.'

'Yet you stayed on at the convent?'

'Yes. I kept hoping that one day God would give me a sign. But he never did.

Or at least, I didn't recognize it.' She paused, troubled by her past indecision, then said: 'But that isn't why I quit.'

He waited and this time she didn't continue. He decided that whatever was chewing at her must be too painful to discuss and started to leave.

'Don't go. Please . . . ' Then as he turned back to her: 'I'm not normally a quitter. In fact once I get my teeth into something I can be most stubborn about not letting go . . . '

Feeling like he was prying, he said: 'You don't have to tell me, Ellie. Not unless you've a mind to.'

She wasn't listening. Her mind was off somewhere, somewhere it didn't want to be, and suddenly she was crying.

Gabriel stood there, absently toeing the ground.

Crying women made him feel awkward. He wanted to comfort them, as he'd seen his father comforting his dying mother and his Sunday-morning flock; but he didn't have his father's passion or gift for words and as a result ended up feeling clumsy and tongue-tied.

He felt that way now. But because Ellen was Cally's sister, he felt strangely linked to her; after a little, for the first time, he was able to overcome his awkwardness. Kneeling, he put his arm around her and stroked her hair.

She responded by burying her face in his chest and sobbing. He tried to soothe her, but soon ran out of words.

Nearby, the stallion stopped grazing and watched Gabriel trying to comfort Ellen. As if understanding his problem, it trotted over and stood close to them, snuffling softly in its nose.

The gentle sound had a positive effect on Ellen. Sniffing back her tears, she gazed up at the Morgan. It wrinkled its lips at her and pawed the ground.

'He isn't going to bite me, is he?'

'Not unless you're fool enough to pet him.'

'Then . . . why's he making that noise?'

Gabriel had no idea — probably just to be ornery, he thought.

'I reckon he's askin' you to stop cryin'.'

As if to verify his words, the stallion snuffled again then whinnied.

'What's he saying now?'

'Tellin' me to shut up.'

Ellen laughed and wiped her eyes with the big red kerchief he offered her.

'You're making all this up, aren't you?'

His wry grin answered her question.

Blowing her nose, she said: 'I don't understand what came over me. Crying like a baby, I should be ashamed of myself.'

'No shame in tears, Ellie. Shame belongs to the folks who cause 'em.'

She smiled and returned his kerchief. 'I'll be all right now. So if you have chores to do, don't let me keep you from them.'

Gabriel hesitated, and she thought he was going to stay. But with a polite tip of his hat he turned and walked up the slope to the cabin.

Ellen regretfully watched him go. She sensed he was hiding the truth from her: that he actually was Mesquite Jennings. But he'd been so kind to her, so honorable in every other way, she couldn't accuse him of lying.

Turning to the stallion, she said: 'If only you could talk. You'd tell me all about him, wouldn't you?'

The Morgan made a gentle snuffling noise. Ellen went to fondle its velvety black nose, then remembering Gabriel's warning jerked her hand back.

The stallion tossed its head and snorted, as if offended, and backed up.

Ellen laughed. 'Oh, so now you want to be petted, do you? Very well. Then get back here. Come on,' she said, offering out her hand. 'Don't be stubborn.'

The Morgan eyed her suspiciously.

'My God,' Ellen said, 'you're just like him. Don't trust anyone, do you?'

As if to dispute that the Morgan trotted up to her, head lowered as if asking to be petted. But just as Ellen tentatively reached out to rub its nose, the horse jerked its head back, neighed shrilly and galloped off.

Ellen watched as it raced around her in a wide circle, prancing and bucking and kicking up its heels in sheer delight.

What a pair they make, she thought. A man and a horse, two of God's creatures, so much alike they could have come from the same mold: two loners, though perhaps not by choice, both suspicious and dangerous in their own way, yet sensitive too, and both as unpredictable as a winter storm.

She watched the stallion for a few more minutes, amused by its antics, then, feeling better, she leaned over the stream and washed away her tears. Refreshed, she patted her face dry with her petticoat and started up the slope, the Morgan trotting behind her like an obedient puppy.

6

Miguel Escalero sat dozing with his back against the cabin wall, his hands clasped around his drawn-up knees, his big frayed sombrero covering him like an umbrella.

He was dreaming of a December Sunday morning many years ago, when as a boy of twelve he'd seen the face of the Madonna smiling at him from the clouds. No one believed him, of course; not even his parents. They just laughed and told him he was imagining things; that it was just the way the clouds were shaped.

But he knew differently; because the Madonna had not only smiled at him, she had spoken to him as well. In a voice like none other he had ever heard, a voice that was so gentle, so soothing it had calmed all his fears, she told him to give his life to God. And when he asked the Madonna if she meant he was to become a padre, she said no, God had plenty of padres; what he needed was someone to help the sisters at the *Convento de Cristo*.

Though surprised that God would ask a boy of his age to do such important work, Miguel knew better than to argue with the Almighty. And that afternoon, after repeating what the Madonna told him to his parents — who also knew better than to argue with God — he left the village and walked the twelve miles to the convent where he offered his services to the *Madre Superiora* — a wise and gentle woman who, after he explained why he was there, and who sent him, seemed most pleased to have his help. After showing him where he could sleep in the stable, she immediately put him to work helping out in the kitchen.

'Miguel . . . Miguel, wake up . . . '

A voice interrupted his dream. Removing his sombrero, he saw it was Ellen.

'Hitch, up the team,' she told him. 'We'll be leaving shortly.'

'*Sí*, Sister.' He rose and plodded off to do her bidding.

Ellen went to the cabin and knocked sharply on the door.

'May I come in, Gabe?'

'The *señor*, he is in the barn,' Escalero called out.

'*Gracias.*'

She found Gabriel cleaning out the Morgan's stall.

'We're going now.'

He accepted the news stoically. 'Always good to get an early start.'

'Yes . . . that's what I thought . . . well, actually it was Miguel's idea. He mentioned it last night and . . . ' her voice trailed off.

Gabriel went on working, at the same time wondering why the idea of her leaving bothered him. He'd thought about it all morning and part of last night too; but he still couldn't decide whether it was because in a few short hours she'd come to mean something to him or because her presence helped him to recapture the love he'd felt for her sister.

'Well,' Ellen was saying, 'I just wanted to thank you for letting us stay and . . . for all you've done for us.'

If he heard her, he showed no sign of it.

'I hope I — we weren't too much of an inconvenience.'

He shook his head without looking up.

Dear God, she thought, getting him to talk is harder than pulling teeth.

'Good,' she heard herself say. 'Then . . . I guess I'll be saying goodbye.' She turned to leave.

'Wait . . . ' Gabriel stopped pitching the hay, leaned on the long-handled fork and studied her with his ice-blue eyes. ''Fore you go, tell me the truth.'

'About what?'

'Why you're lookin' for Mesquite Jennings.'

'What difference would that make?'

'None, most likely. But I'd still like to know.'

She hesitated, then locked gazes with him.

'You're a gunfighter, aren't you?'

His eyes narrowed but he didn't reply.

'You're a strange man, Gabe. You expect me to tell you the truth yet you won't even admit what you are.'

He sighed heavily. 'Sure,' he admitted. 'I carry a gun and I've used it to kill men. Most of 'em deserved it but not all. Some just had too much whiskey in 'em. Others just picked the wrong man to argue with.'

'And you killed them all?'

His silence assured her that he had.

'And I suppose you're going to say it was you or them?'

More silence.

'Couldn't you have just walked away?'

'Not unless I planned on spendin' the rest of my life holed up in a cave.'

'Isn't that what you're doing now, hiding out here, in the middle of nowhere, rather than face the music?'

'Dancin' at the end of a rope isn't my idea of music, Sister Kincaide.' He went back to cleaning out the stall. 'Now, you can tell me your story or cut dust, makes no matter to me.'

She took a deep breath to steady herself, and then said:

'There's a man, a very powerful man, a rancher who has more land and more cattle than all the other ranchers in New Mexico combined and yet he still wants more. He rules Santa Rosa and all the land for miles around like a medieval king. He bribes senators, puts judges in office, and tells sheriffs what to do.'

'Stadtlander. Stillman J. Stadtlander.'

'Then you know him?'

'We've crossed trails.'

'And you're still alive? I'm impressed.'

'Don't be. Like you said: I'm the one hidin' out down here.'

There was shame in his voice as if he hated himself for running away. Wishing now she hadn't mentioned it, she said:

'I only met Mr Stadtlander once

— at a square dance in Las Cruces. He came up to me and said how much he respected my grandfather. I was too intimidated to answer and that amused him. He said he guessed Grampa Tate had told me how they'd butted heads in the past, but not to hold it against him because he would never try to run roughshod over Grandfather again. Then he kissed my hand and walked off. Later I asked Grampa Tate about him and he made a face and spat as if to get rid of a bad taste in his mouth. Then he called Mr Stadtlander some names he'd never used in front of me before and stormed off. I never mentioned Mr Stadtlander to him again.' She paused and sighed. 'I guess he wasn't born evil, though some folks say he was. But greed and the love of power, along with losing his wife and only daughter to consumption changed him — turned him into the ruthless bully he is now.'

Gabriel didn't say anything. He could have told Ellen a lot more about

Stillman Stadtlander, most of it bad, but not without revealing more of himself than he wanted her to know. So he said quietly:

'You still haven't told me what happened to make you quit the convent.'

'He — Mr Stadtlander browbeat a bunch of witnesses into lying to save his son, Slade, from going to prison, maybe even the gallows.'

'Nothin' new about that, Ellie. He's been bailing his boy out of trouble since Slade fell from the cradle.'

'I don't care about all those other times,' Ellen said bitterly. 'I just want Slade and that Iverson trash he runs with to pay for killing my sister.'

'Cally's dead? When?'

'Three weeks ago. Three weeks and two days, to be precise.'

'How? What happened?'

'Slade and Mace and Cody Iverson got drunk one night in her cantina. They started breaking up the place and Cally told them to leave. When they wouldn't, she got the shotgun she keeps under the bar and kicked them out. She thought that was the end of it. But they waited for her and after she'd closed up and was walking home, they grabbed her and dragged her into a gully where they . . . they took turns raping her and . . . and . . . then they killed her and left her for the coyotes.'

Gabriel felt a cold rage erupt inside him.

'Of course, they denied it. Claimed that after they left the cantina they rode back to the ranch and played poker until sunup.'

'And the law believed them?'

'Why not? Sheriff Forbes has been on Mr Stadtlander's payroll for years. Everyone knows that. Plus there were a dozen or more witnesses who swore Slade and the Iversons never left the bunkhouse all night.'

'Witnesses who ride for the Double SS?'

'Naturally.'

'Damn,' Gabriel said softly.

Both were silent a moment. Then:

'I never thought I could wish another person dead,' Ellen said bitterly. 'But now, I swear to God I could pull the trap myself and watch all three of them dancing their way to hell.'

Gabriel felt the same way.

'And what you just told me, you know it to be gospel?'

Ellen nodded. 'One night about two weeks ago Cody got drunk in the Copper Palace and bragged about how he and his brother held Cally down while Slade . . . Slade . . . ' she broke off, unable to finish.

Gabriel pulled her close and held her tightly against him.

'It's all right,' she assured him. 'I'm not going to fall apart again. I'm not going to cry either. I'm all cried out. Now all I feel is hate. That's why I had to leave the convent. You cannot feel as I do and give your life to God. God is merciful and he expects his children to be merciful; to forgive others their sins as he forgives us ours. But I can't forgive. I've tried, God knows I've tried. But then I think of Cally, of how much she suffered, and all I want is revenge . . . to see the three of them die.'

Gabriel nodded, understanding.

'An' you figure if you find Mesquite Jennings, he'll help you?'

'I'm hoping. He's a shootist, and from what everybody says as cold-blooded and deadly as they come. If anyone can kill Slade and the Iversons, it's him.'

'But why would he want to? Ever ask yourself that?'

'For revenge.'

'Yours or his?'

'Both.'

He frowned, not convinced.

'Five years is a long time to keep a hate boilin'. 'Least, it would be for me.'

'I don't know how to respond to that.'

Normally he would have let the matter drop. But for some unknown reason her disappointment made him feel guilty and he felt obliged to defend himself.

'You're forgettin' somethin', Ellie. Even if Jennings did your killin' that wouldn't be the end of it. Stadtlander would come after him an' then he'd have to take down the old man too. And with twenty or thirty saddle tramps backing Stadtlander's play, the odds of Jennings comin' out on top ain't in his favor.'

'The odds weren't in favor of David slaying Goliath either. But it happened. And I believe it can happen again. It has to. It's the only way justice will be served.'

Gabriel saw a look in Ellen's violet eyes he didn't like.

'There's somethin' you're not tellin' me. What is it?'

She hesitated before saying: 'Jennings and Cally were more than just sweethearts. Their love was special. Cally told me so. Said if he hadn't been what he was, and she'd been willing to live on the run, they would have gotten married.'

'An' you believed her?'

'Why shouldn't I? Cally and I didn't always agree on everything, especially when it came to her choice of men or the way she ran her life. But I don't believe she ever knowingly lied to me.'

Gabriel decided not to press the issue.

'An' you're hopin' that when Jennings finds out Cally was raped an' killed, he'll remember how much he loved her an' risk his life to gun these skunks down?'

'Wouldn't you?'

'I've never loved anyone that much.'

'I don't believe that.'

'Meaning?'

Calling on all her courage Ellen said: 'You're Mesquite Jennings. You know it and I know it. So stop lying to me.'

His pale blue eyes turned flinty.

'Lucky you're a woman — '

'Oh, please,' she said, losing her patience. 'Don't threaten me. We both know you're not going to shoot me, regardless of what I say.'

Her audacity floored him.

'You got sand, I'll give you that.'

'Enough to make you change your mind?'

His tight-lipped silence told her no.

'Why not? Do you deny you loved my sister?'

More tight-lipped silence.

'Yet you won't destroy the men who killed her?'

He met her gaze and held it.

'Love can stir a man to do many things,' he said quietly, 'but deliberately stickin' his head in a noose ain't one of 'em.'

'I'll pay you,' she said desperately. 'As much as you want. In gold!'

He studied her, eyes full of questions.

'I'm not lying. I sold the cantina. It didn't bring as much as I hoped, but I'll wager it's enough to persuade you to kill Slade and the Iversons.'

'You'd lose that bet, Ellie.' He looked about him. 'This place ain't much, but it's enough for me. I know how to die standing up. An' when it's time, this is where I'll do it.'

She sighed, defeated.

'Go home,' he said gently. 'Mexico's no place for you. It's still wild, like Texas an' New Mexico were thirty years ago. It's got mountains so high they polish the sun and deserts that suck the life out of a man. Take my advice. Go back to Las Cruces. Bury your pain. Find a fella who'll treat you well an' help you raise some young'uns. Make your life worthwhile. You deserve it.'

'And Cally — what does she deserve?'

'Cally's dead,' he said simply. 'Nothin' can change that.'

'But avenging her death would make life less of a hell.'

He shrugged, not willing to argue.

'One last piece of advice, Ellie: You have to go through San Dimas on your way home. If you talk to anyone, don't be mentionin' gold. They might figure you got it with you. Then your life an' the old man's won't last longer than summer lightning.' He leaned the pitchfork against the stall and walked out before she could stop him.

7

Gabriel caught up with Escalero as he was returning uphill from the stream. He had two heavy, dripping canvas water bags slung over his shoulders. Gabriel took one and helped the old man rope them to the side of the wagon.

Neither spoke until they were sure the bags were secure; then Gabriel asked Escalero if he had a weapon.

'*Sí, señor. Una pistola.*'

'Mind if I take a look at it?'

'It would be my honor — Señor Jennings.' Escalero pulled a gun from under his loose-fitting shirt and handed it, butt first, to Gabriel. As he did he looked intently at the gunfighter, his calm, unflinching gaze telling Gabriel that he had not survived all these years by being unobservant.

Gabriel smiled grimly.

'How long you known, *compadre?*'

'Since from the beginning, *señor* — when I first stopped the wagon and saw you. These eyes, they may be old and no longer able to see an eagle on high, but they do not forget a face.'

'You've seen me before?'

'*Sí, señor.*'

'Where? When?'

'One night. Outside La Casa Vega.'

'Las Cruces? That's been a spell. You got a powerful memory, *hombre.*'

'This is one memory I wish to forget,' Escalero said sadly. 'I am but a grain of sand in God's eyes, yet I know it is wrong to take the life of another — for any reason.'

Gabriel shrugged, neither agreeing nor disagreeing.

'Sometimes,' he said softly, 'things happen for no reason. They just happen. Who knows why? Fella gets an itch. Has to scratch it. Calls you out. Slaps leather. It's him or you. I make no excuse for bein' faster.'

'Nor do I pass judgment on another man's deed.'

'That why you haven't told the

señorita who I am?'

'No, *señor*. I have not informed Sister Kincaide because I do not wish her to hire you — you or any other *pistolero* who is willing to kill these men for her. No good can come of it.'

'Well, 'least we agree on one thing,' Gabriel said. 'But you don't have to worry about me.'

'You are all done with killing, *señor?*'

Gabriel nodded. 'An' there's nothin' I can think of could make me go back to it again.'

As if suddenly remembering the gun in his hand, he now examined it. It was an old 1860 Army Colt single shot pistol. The grips were missing, the screws holding the brass trigger guard in place were loose and the firing pin was worn.

'When's the last time you fired this?'

'Not so recently, *señor.*'

'Figures.' Gabriel pulled the 1890 Remington .44–40 from his Levis. The gun was only a year old and he'd paid extra to have a gunsmith engrave his initials on the left side plate.

'Here, take this.' He handed the revolver to Escalero.

'What about you, *señor?*'

'I got the Winchester. An' if need be, I can always pick up another handgun next time I'm in San Dimas.'

'*Muches gracias, señor.* It is most gracious of you.'

'Let's hope you never have to use it, *compadre.*' Gabriel took a handful of cartridges from his belt and gave them to Escalero. The old Mexican placed them carefully in the storage box under the wagon seat. Then they stood with their backs to the sun talking about where the next water could be found, what the chances were of it being dried up or poisoned with alkali, and on which sections of the trail to San Dimas to be on the lookout for bandits.

'If these hellions do jump you,' Gabriel concluded, 'they'll come out of the sun hopin' the glare will blind you. So be sure an' keep your hat pulled down over your eyes an' aim for the horses — '

'The horses, *señor?*'

'Sure. They're a bigger target. 'Sides, around here horses are hard to come by. And a bandit without a horse ain't worth pissin' on. I know it goes against the grain,' Gabriel said as the old Mexican looked uncomfortable, 'but remember, you got a woman to protect. An' keepin' her away from those gutless sons-of-bitches is worth more than a few horses.'

'Do not worry, *señor.* I will defend her with my life.'

'I never figured differently, *amigo.*' Gabriel paused as he saw Ellen emerge from the cabin then said softly, so only Escalero could hear: 'Keep this between us, OK? No reason to throw a scare into her.'

Escalero looked offended. '*No soy un hombre que chismes, señor.*'

Gabriel grinned, amused by the old man's saltiness. 'I wasn't suggestin' you're a gossip, *amigo*, I just meant this is strictly our business. *Hombre a hombre. Comprendo?*'

Escalero nodded, bowed his apologies and turned his attention to the mules. He was some old Mexican.

Meanwhile, Gabriel watched Ellen approach. He noticed she had pinned her veil up and despite her grim black attire, looked uncommonly pretty in the morning light. He liked the way she walked, too — like a spring colt prancing in a pasture or a young girl hurrying home from school.

Carrying the earthenware bowl of fresh eggs and the last of the biscuits he'd earlier insisted she take with her, Ellen let Gabriel help her onto the wagon. She then thanked him again for his hospitality.

He heard the disappointment in her voice. It cut deep and for an instant he considered changing his mind. Ellen must have sensed he was wavering because she continued to look hopefully at him, all the time praying he'd offer to go with her.

When he didn't she sagged as if all life had been sucked from her. Then, turning to Escalero, she sadly told him to get started.

The old Mexican slapped the mules with the reins and urged them forward. The wagon creaked and rattled as it rolled away.

★　★　★

Gabriel shaded his eyes with his hat and watched them drive off. He felt as if a part of him was leaving with them.

Ahead of the plodding mules, at the far end of the valley, the trail forked: one route led to the desert and eventually San Dimas, the other climbed into the scorched foothills and then continued on up, higher and higher, finally reaching the Sierra Madre Occidental: massive, rugged, untamed mountains fraught with danger.

Gabriel sighed and toed the dirt with his boot. For the second time in his life, he knew he was losing someone important. Worse, for the second time he had chosen not to do anything about it. Could it be he wasn't the man he hoped he was? Had his father's prophecy finally come true?

'Son,' he'd said on the day Gabriel told him he was striking out on his own, 'the path you're taking is not a righteous one: it is leading you away from the Good Book.'

'Pa, if God is the Almighty, the way you keep sayin' he is, then he should be all around us — everywhere. An' if he's everywhere then I shouldn't have no trouble findin' him when I need him.'

'You keep packing that iron on your hip, boy, an' you're gonna need him all the time.'

'Not if I'm fast enough,' Gabriel replied. 'An' I'm plenty fast.'

His father, his low resonant voice sounding just as spiritual as it did at prayer meetings, said:

'Son, I know I can't change your mind. Only your ma could do that and she's in higher hands now. But you hear me, boy. Hear me good. Gonna come a day when being fast with a gun won't help you. Then you'll find out what kind of man you truly are.'

And now, today, Gabriel thought as he again absently toed the ground, he had found out.

God damn that ol' man's soul, he thought angrily. Then, immediately feeling ashamed for speaking ill of his father, he silently apologized and let his mind wander back to Cally.

Memories of their brief time together flooded his mind. Oh, how he'd loved her and how she had loved him. And though that was five years ago and he'd long since gotten over losing her, encountering Ellen had brought those memories to the forefront and he realized they were as painful as ever.

So, why hadn't he gone with her?

Common sense told him that he'd made the right choice; but deep down, where a man can't lie to himself, he knew that his fear of hanging shouldn't have stopped him; he knew his failure to measure up would always haunt him.

Heavy-hearted, he trudged to the cabin.

On the way he passed the barn. His footsteps brought the stallion charging to the door. It snorted, tossing its proud head and pawing the dirt as if challenging him to dare enter its domain.

Pissed off, Gabriel picked up a stone and threw it at the Morgan. It hit the horse on its flank, stinging it, causing it to flinch. It reared up, angrily pawing the air and neighing shrilly. Then as Gabriel continued on to the cabin, the stallion suddenly charged him.

Gabriel heard the horse coming. It wasn't the first time the Morgan had attacked him. He had scars to prove that. Not wanting any more, he sprinted to the cabin and got inside before the stallion could bite him.

Safely indoors, Gabriel looked out of the window and saw the all-black Morgan raging up and down in front of the door.

If I didn't need you so much, you miserable lop-eared bastard, he thought, I'd shoot you right between the goddamn eyes.

8

He did not sleep well that night. Ghosts of the past haunted his dreams and he was still troubled by them when morning came.

He crossed to the stove, listlessly stirred the embers and began breakfast. But he had little appetite and taking his plate outside, he walked around back and dumped most of his scrambled eggs, bacon and fried potatoes on the ground for the scavengers. Next he washed himself in the basin on the rock behind the cabin, lathering his face before shaving in the piece of cracked mirror that he balanced up against the wall. The straight-edge he'd stolen from a barbershop soon after escaping from the boys' reformatory in El Paso seemed as dull as his spirits. He honed it on the old leather strap dangling from a nearby nail then carefully finished shaving. But he still nicked himself.

He squinted at his reflection in the mirror — a reflection that was backed by a cloudless, lemony-blue sky — watching as a tiny bubble of blood welled up on his chin. He dabbed it with the towel, staining one corner; then, too depressed to care about the glory of the day or the caracaras circling hungrily overhead, he dumped out the soapy water and walked around to the front of the cabin.

That was when he noticed the barn door was open. He realized he must have not locked it last night. Not that it mattered. The stallion could have kicked the door down any time it felt like it. Locking the Morgan up at night was merely Gabriel's way of reminding it of who was boss, just as the stallion sometimes bucked him off for the same reason. It was a game they played to keep each other alert and in check; a game that both man and horse accepted without rancor.

Once inside the cabin Gabriel dressed and brushed his hair. A smear of blood on his palm reminded him that his chin was still bleeding. He splashed a little whiskey onto the towel and pressed it against the cut. It stung momentarily, but satisfied his concern about infection. He went to cork the bottle but instead impulsively took a swig. The whiskey warmed his belly and made him feel better. He took another swig, then another, and another until eventually he felt pretty damned good. He chuckled, amused for no reason, and on hearing the stallion neighing went to the window and looked out.

Brandy limped up to the door, favoring his right foreleg. Gabriel went out and studied the horse, wondering whether there was something really wrong with the leg or if it was the whiskey playing tricks with his mind. No, he thought, the leg or his hoof is definitely bothering him. Warily approaching the Morgan, which never moved but watched him with its fierce dark eyes, he knelt, lifted the leg and examined the hoof. Seeing no stone or thorn lodged there, Gabriel set the hoof down and gently felt around the leg, first checking the fetlock, then the cannon and lastly the knee.

Finding nothing wrong he straightened up and walked slowly around the stallion. Still no sign of physical problems. Returning to his original position, Gabriel shook his head, baffled.

'What the hell's wrong with you?' he asked, thinking aloud more than actually talking to the horse. The stallion snuffled softly and nudged Gabriel's arm with its nose.

Suspicious of the Morgan's gentleness, Gabriel warily rubbed its forehead and spoke soothingly to it. At the same time, he grasped the thick black mane and tried to lead it forward. Let's see you walk, he thought. Then maybe I can get some idea of what's ailing you.

But the stallion jerked free, and lowering its head playfully butted him in the chest sending him stumbling backward. As he sat down hard on the step the horse reared up, pawing at the air and whinnying.

Thinking he was going to be stomped, Gabriel raised his arms to protect himself and rolled sideways. But the flailing hoofs never touched him. Instead, the Morgan whirled and galloped off, head raised, neck proudly arched, long tail feathering in the wind.

Gabriel watched, agape, as the obviously uninjured stallion leaped the corral fence and pranced joyfully around in a circle.

Son-of-a-gun, he thought, as he realized there was nothing wrong with the horse. That black devil's been jerking my tail!

9

The day passed slowly. He had no idea why, but he felt like it was the lull before the storm.

To keep his mind off Ellen he spent all morning catching up on his chores. There were chickens and pigs to feed (the goats ate whatever they found on the hillsides), eggs to collect and a cabin to sweep out. When he was done, he saw the wood for the stove had gotten low, so he brought in more from the pile behind the cabin. He then entered the barn, intending to clean the stallion's stall. But the Morgan had apparently forgotten its moment of gentleness and tried to cow-kick him every time he got close. Gabriel threw the broom at the horse and plodded back to the cabin, thinking, Damn him, he can clean the stall himself.

By now the sun was almost directly

overhead. Hungry, he wolfed down three hard-boiled eggs, a cold ham steak and a bowl of refried beans. As he ate in the silence of the cabin, a silence he had never noticed before, he realized there was a big difference between being alone and being lonely. He'd been alone most of his life, but seldom lonely. Now, he missed Ellen. And not, he realized, because she reminded him of Cally. But because in a few short hours she had made such a positive impression on him that without her his life seemed empty. It was an ugly feeling and he again regretted not helping her.

When he'd finished eating he chased his meal down with a shot of J. H. Cutter. He was not much of a day-drinker, especially when he was alone, but the whiskey boosted his sagging spirits.

Whistling, he went out and worked in the vegetable patch all afternoon, weeding, planting black-bean seeds, watering his onions, chayote squash, bell peppers, and flowering jalapeño vines. In the oven-hot sun it was hard, back-breaking work, especially lugging buckets of water up from the stream, and when he stopped at sunset he was worn out and soaked with sweat.

After cooling off in the stream he returned to the cabin and fixed a meal out of his lunch leftovers.

After supper, he lit a cigar and sat on the doorstep sipping his whiskey while watching a swarm of bats hunting insects in the darkening sky.

Dusk gradually chased away the last light. Insects whined past his ears in the darkness. A sickle moon and endless stars brightened the indigo sky. Presently, a cool breeze swept down off the Sierras. Gabriel pulled up his shirt collar and drank from the bottle. Mind drifting, he spat out a smoke-ring and idly poked a finger through it. The whiskey and a full stomach made him sleepy. His eyelids grew leaden and gradually he dozed off.

Out of nowhere Cally's face appeared. She smiled and said something he couldn't hear. She looked exactly as she had when he'd ridden off that night, only minutes ahead of a posse, leaving her standing in the cantina doorway, her lovely face and long autumn-gold hair glinting in the lamplight. He'd promised her that he would be back, no matter what, and she'd smiled that sad little smile of hers and waved goodbye. He had meant what he said, but like so many other outlaws on the run, his destiny was decided for him.

Gabriel's dream was suddenly interrupted by a shrill neigh. He looked up just in time to see the Morgan burst out of the barn, already at full gallop, and charge off down the slope into the darkness.

Gabriel wondered what had startled the stallion. Ten years ago it might have been a band of hostiles after livestock, or marauding Comancheros down from west Texas, the mixture of renegade whites and liquored-up Comanches ready to rob, rape or kill anyone they came upon; but now, in the summer of '91, those types of raids were a thing of the past. Even attacks by border trash were rare. *Bandidos* were all a person had to worry about these days. And generally they stayed in the mountains, ambushing travelers rather than wandering out into the open and risking a fight with the well-armed *Rurales*.

Still, something had frightened Brandy and Gabriel decided to investigate. Armed with his Winchester and a lamp, he crossed to the barn. Empty. Wondering if the unpredictable horse was playing games with him again, he decided to take advantage of its absence and clean out the stall. He hung the lamp on a hook, he grabbed the pitchfork and began removing the soiled straw.

At that moment the stallion returned. Gabriel heard its hoofs clatter into the barn and whirled, pitchfork raised to keep it away.

'Get outta here!' he yelled. 'Y' hear me? Go on! *Vamos!*'

But the Morgan was already charging. It swerved past the fork, slamming into Gabriel and sending him sprawling. From the floor he saw the enraged stallion rear up, screaming, forelegs flailing, and knew his time had come. But the descending hoofs weren't aimed at him; instead they pounded at something under the straw in the stall. Again and again the stallion stamped the straw. Then at last it stopped and stood there, snorting.

Shaken, Gabriel slowly got up and stared at the trembling stallion.

'Whoa, easy now, fella, easy . . . '

He inched past the agitated horse and saw the dead sidewinder curled amongst the straw, its horned head and fat body mashed by the flailing hoofs.

'Judas H. Priest.' Gabriel whistled softly and looked at Brandy. The Morgan had calmed down. Realizing that he owed the horse an apology, maybe even his life, he reached out to rub the stallion's soft black nose — then jerked his hand back, just in time to avoid getting bitten.

'Why, you ornery sonofa . . . ' Gabriel grabbed the lamp and stormed past the fiery-eyed Morgan.

As he was leaving, Gabriel saw a bucket sitting by the door. He grabbed it, hurled it at the horse and ran out. Nor did he stop running until he was safely in the cabin. There, after catching his breath, he went to the window and looked out.

The stallion stood in the doorway of the barn, silhouetted against the moon. It looked nothing short of magnificent and Gabriel couldn't help admiring it.

The more things change, he thought wryly, the more they stay the same.

He went to bed.

10

He awoke some time in the night, disturbed by something moving behind the cabin. At first he thought it might be the stallion — though he knew the Morgan seldom left the barn at night — or maybe a coyote on the prowl. Then he heard it again, recognized the familiar crunching sound made by human beings creeping along in boots and knew instinctively that the bounty hunters had returned.

He pulled on his boots, took down the Winchester and quietly levered a shell into the chamber. He then waited, motionless, ears straining to pinpoint where each of his attackers were.

One — no, two were approaching the door. He couldn't place the third man and wondered whether he was after the stallion or hiding in the darkness somewhere, rifle trained on the door in case Gabriel got past his companions.

Deciding that caution was the way, Gabriel crouched behind the table, ready to gun down anyone who tried to enter. It wouldn't be easy for them. Stout blocks of wood, slid each night into place, kept the door and the window shutters barred. Nothing short of dynamite or a battering ram could break them open.

Suddenly a lamp smashed against the door. Gabriel heard glass shatter, smelled kerosene and realized they intended to burn him out.

Not waiting for the inevitable, he grabbed the blanket off his bed, dunked it in the bucket of water by the stove and wrapped it around himself. By now the door was aflame and he could hear the stallion neighing shrilly in the barn.

He unbarred the door, jerked it open and threw the chair out first, drawing the bounty hunters' fire. He then dived outside, hitting the ground and rolling over, firing at the two human silhouettes he saw outlined against the crackling blaze.

One man gave a yelp and limped off into the darkness; the other took cover behind the corral fence. Gabriel jumped up and, keeping low, ran for the barn.

A shot fired from a higher angle nicked Gabriel on his left arm, forcing him to hit the dirt. He knew now that the third man was among the rocks atop the slope, and rolling over he squeezed off two quick rounds. The bullets ricocheted off the rocks, making the sniper duck his head. Gabriel took a chance, jumped up, and dove into the barn.

Bullets plunked into the door dangerously near his head. He returned fire, aiming directly at the flashes, and heard a grunt of pain.

Men's voices whispered to each other in the darkness. He couldn't hear what was being said, but a few moments later he heard horses galloping away.

He waited, hearing the stallion stirring restlessly behind him. When he was satisfied the bounty hunters weren't returning, he sat up and faced the Morgan. The horse was glaring at him over the side of the stall. Its eyes were two fiery red glints. Gabriel laughed softly to himself. The goddamn brute was more angry than scared!

Then he smelled smoke and remembered the fire. He jumped up, ran out into the moonlight and saw that the flames were licking up onto the roof. Gabriel ran to the water barrel, filled a bucket and tried to douse them.

He made numerous trips but eventually he had to face it: the cabin was ablaze and there was no saving it. Lungs choked with smoke, he stood back and bitterly watched the last two years of his life burn to a blackened skeleton.

He didn't hear the stallion trot up beside him. Nor did he bother to look at it as he said grimly:

'Horse, it's time you an' me rode north.'

11

At dawn the next morning, before the rooster stopped crowing, Gabriel left the barn where he'd slept and breakfasted on four raw eggs and a gourd of goat's milk. He then released the pigs and goats so they could fend for themselves, and left the barn door open so the chickens could wander in and out.

Next he walked halfway down the slope to a pile of rocks and rolled one aside. Beneath it was a bundle wrapped in an old slicker. He unfolded it and took out the contents: a bedroll, canteen, a box of 44–40 cartridges. He'd buried everything right after he'd taken possession of the abandoned cabin for the very reason he was now going to need them: survival.

Only this time he wouldn't be battling just lawmen or bounty hunters;

this time he'd be up against a far more powerful enemy, a man everyone feared, a man he'd once admired, even thought of as a surrogate father: Stillman J. Stadtlander.

Gabriel pocketed the cartridges, filled the canteen from the stream, walked back up the slope to the Morgan and tied the bedroll behind his saddle. Then he mounted and rode off without once looking back at the smoldering remains of the cabin.

His arm ached where the bullet had nicked him, but the bleeding had stopped shortly after he'd poured the last of the whiskey on it and now, except for some stiffness, it worked fine.

He rode out across the flat scrubland, the stallion's easy lope giving him the sense of being in a rocking-chair. In the cool dry air the Morgan was capable of keeping the pace steady for mile after mile. But Gabriel, sensing he hadn't seen the last of the bounty hunters, reined the horse in as soon as they reached the end of the valley.

Ahead, the trail climbed through several big rocky outcrops, then sloped down into a vast desert of greasewood and *cholla*. The latter, a cactus that grew in strange, twisty shapes, was covered with sharp clingy spines that stuck to boots and clothing and were painful as hell to dig out once they got under the skin.

It was getting hot and Gabriel slowed the Morgan to a walk. To cross the desert in summer heat was dangerous, often fatal. Known as *Viaje del Muerto*, or Dead Man's Journey, the land seemed harmless enough until one noticed the numerous bleached-white bones poking up through the reddish dirt. Rider and horse had to be especially careful where they trod, as stones and ruts and pockets of quick-sand could cause a broken leg or a twisted ankle — dooming the victim, man or beast, to eventually die of dehydration.

But today Gabriel knew he had more to worry about than the desert. As he rode slowly across the wasteland he rested the Winchester across his arm, ready to fire at anything threatening.

After an hour or so he approached a mile-long gully walled on both sides by boulders. His intuition honed by a life on the run, he knew this was where the bushwhacking would take place. Glancing up at the sun he saw that it glared down on his left side. Now he knew where the bounty hunters would be hiding. But from high up and at so steep an angle, it wouldn't be an easy shot.

Making a run for it was out of the question: even if they missed him with every shot they might still hit the horse. And once he was on foot they could wait him out until he died of thirst.

It was then that he remembered a coyote he'd once hunted. The wily creature had kept exposing itself for a second before ducking out of sight. Each time Gabriel fired at it and missed. It was a daring ruse but it worked. After a dozen shots, Gabriel decided to look for easier game and gave up. The coyote's mocking yip-yipping had rung in his ears as he rode off.

Now, hoping that the bounty hunters were watching, he dismounted and examined the stallion's left foreleg. Then pretending the horse had gone lame, he switched the rifle to his right hand, grasped the reins with his left and started walking.

To make himself less of a target he kept changing his pace from fast to slow, slow to fast, now and then weaving and stumbling as if fatigued by the heat.

He'd covered about fifty yards when a shot rang out. The bullet grazed his shoulder, and before there was time for another shot Gabriel whacked the Morgan with the rifle butt and dived behind the nearest rock. The startled horse galloped off along the gully before the bounty hunters could shoot it.

Relieved, Gabriel kept ducked down

as a steady hail of bullets chipped the rock near his head. Eventually, when the firing stopped, he poked his head up for a second, then ducked down again, drawing another volley of rifle fire. He repeated the maneuver several times, each time getting a glimpse of where the three men were hiding.

When the next lull came he had his target already marked. Quickly resting the Winchester atop the rock, he took aim and fired three rounds.

There was a sharp cry and a body tumbled down, bouncing from rock to rock until it landed in a heap on the dirt. It was the youngest of the three bounty hunters, and his enraged father jumped up and pumped round after round at Gabriel.

Gabriel eased over behind the next rock, took careful aim and dropped the older man. He then stood up, and blazed away at the remaining son. Panicking, the bounty hunter scrambled over the rocks until a bullet in the head cut him down.

Gabriel watched him stagger and fall. His body slid limply down the steep rocky slope and landed in a heap in the gully. Feeling no remorse, Gabriel left the three bodies for the buzzards, shouldered his rifle and plodded on down the gully.

He found the stallion waiting about a hundred yards off. It snorted and gave him a look that showed how pissed off it was that he had whacked it. Gabriel knew that look and kept his rifle ready in case the Morgan tried to bite him. It didn't. Gabriel swung up into the saddle, gripped the horn and spurred the horse forward — expecting it to buck. Again, nothing happened.

'Don't think you're foolin' me,' Gabriel told the stallion as they rode off. ''Cause I'll be burning in the fires of hell 'fore I believe you've gone soft.'

12

Every summer San Dimas, a remote sun-baked pueblo in north-west Chihuahua, earned its nickname *El horno del diablo*, the devil's furnace. Trapped between the Sierra Madre and the towering, sheer walls of the *Cañon Solo*, the town was plagued by scaring winds off the desert that kept the air so stifling hot it burned the lungs. If that wasn't enough, temperatures regularly soared above a hundred degrees and often stayed that way for weeks at a time.

Today was no exception. As Gabriel rode in from the desert, the sun hammered down on him, making breathing an effort.

On the outskirts he passed an old man, face hidden beneath a tattered straw hat, leading a *burro* loaded down with firewood. The man acknowledged him with a courteous nod and plodded on. On both sides of him white-shirted *campesinos* toiled in the bean fields, their heads shielded from the merciless sun by huge straw sombreros. Gabriel returned their waves and rode on, thinking how much he respected these gentle, compassionate people.

Ahead, women with bright-colored shawls over their heads sat in the doorways of hovels, grinding corn to make tortillas. They watched stoically as Gabriel rode past.

Their grubby, half-naked children weren't so reserved. As soon as he approached they stopped playing in the dirt and came running up, hands outstretched to him, pleading for pesos.

Gabriel knew if he gave them money they would follow him everywhere. But he couldn't resist their insistent pleas and tossed them a few coins. As they scrambled in the dirt for them, he spat out the dead cigar he'd been chewing, licked his parched lips for the umpteenth time and spurred the stallion into a canter, leaving the children behind.

He followed a narrow dirt street lined with old adobe dwellings into the plaza. A spear of welcome shade cast by the church bell tower temporarily soothed Gabriel's squinted eyes. But moments later he was back in the sunlight, the glare doubly bright now, making him pull his hat lower over his eyes.

He rode on, skirting a pigeon-stained statue of President Porfirio Diaz, and crossed the plaza. Ever wary when among strangers, he noticed that the shops around him were open but the intense heat was preventing anyone from using them.

Neither could he see anybody working inside the office of the local *Rurales*, or any saddled horses tied up outside. In fact, other than a young woman nursing her baby beside a vegetable stand and two bare-footed children carrying urns full of water, the sun-scorched square was deserted.

Gabriel reined up at the livery stable

and told the hostler to 'Grain him.' Then he pulled his Winchester from its boot and asked the sleepy youth if he'd seen a gringo woman, dressed all in black, with an old Mexican driving a wagon. 'They would've ridden in some time the day before yesterday,' he added, 'most likely late in the afternoon.'

The hostler shook his head. He'd seen no one like that. And he would have remembered them, he said, because he'd seen them earlier in the week when they drove in from the border.

Puzzled, Gabriel asked him if he'd heard anyone talking about them. The hostler shook his head again, yawned and led the Morgan away to feed it.

Concerned for Ellen's and Escalero's safety, Gabriel left the stable and crossed over to *El Tecolote*.

Inside, the cantina was not much cooler. A small boy with enormous black eyes sat in the corner under an old stuffed owl, tugging on a string tied to a ceiling fan. Its creaking, slow-turning blades brought the smell of greasy cooking from the kitchen in back.

Gabriel leaned on the bar and waited to be served. There were several other customers, all of them Mexicans. Gabriel recognized them from previous visits and knew they meant him no harm. He asked them the same question he'd asked the hostler. They all shook their heads and went on talking.

Just then the owner, Ramon Salazar, emerged from the kitchen with plates of tortillas, eggs and refried beans. After serving them to the men, along with bowls of chili sauce, he waddled fatly up to Gabriel. Without being asked, he poured Gabriel a whiskey and asked him what he wanted to eat.

'Same as them,' Gabriel said, thumbing at the other customers. He then questioned Salazar about Ellen and Escalero. But the owner hadn't seen them either, and he waddled back into the kitchen.

Gabriel gulped his drink, poured

himself another and tried to reassure himself that Ellie was safe. But since this was the only direct route to the border, and an easy trail to follow, he couldn't convince himself that no harm had come to her.

He was halfway through his meal and still trying to decide what to do next when he heard horses reining up outside. Turning to the window, he saw it was the local *Rurales* — six enlisted men and an officious, mustachioed captain named Plaxido Morales. They all looked hot and weary from their long, hard ride. Their faces were sweat-caked, and their distinctive gray, silver-braided uniforms, red ties and big fancy sombreros were coated with dust.

Before Gabriel could figure out what they were up to, Captain Morales and his men burst into the cantina and aimed their rifles at him.

'*Espere! Sostenga su fuego!*' Gabriel yelled and quickly raised his hands. '*Qué pasa?*' he then asked Captain Morales. 'What's goin' on?'

'You are under arrest, gringo!'
'For what?'

Lights exploded before his eyes as Captain Morales struck him in the face with his pistol. Stunned, Gabriel dropped his Winchester and collapsed to his knees. As if from a distance he heard Captain Morales ordering his men to take him to jail.

13

Gabriel sat on the bunk in the grim little cell and tried to collect his thoughts. It wasn't easy. His face was bruised, lips swollen and his head throbbed with pain. And the heat, my God the heat was suffocating.

But bad as the heat was, the horseflies were worse. Their vicious bites kept him squirming. He swatted at them with his hat, wondering as he did why he'd been treated so harshly. Captain Morales had seen him many times before when he'd come to town and there'd never been a problem.

'You! Gringo!'

Gabriel saw Captain Morales standing on the other side of the bars. The officer was holding a 44–40 Remington revolver. As Gabriel rose and came close he recognized it, and realized Ellie and Escalero must be in trouble.

'This *pistola* — it is yours, yes?'

'Yeah. Those are my initials, see,' Gabriel pointed at the side plate. 'How'd you get hold of it?'

'I will ask the questions, *hombre*.'

Gabriel waited.

'The *Señorita*,' Captain Morales said, 'the *norteamericano* with the pale hair cut so short, what have you done with her?'

'Nothin'. Why?'

'Do not bother to lie. I found this,' he brandished the 44–40 Remington, 'beside her overturned wagon.'

'That's 'cause I gave it to her driver, Miguel Escalero, for protection against *bandidos*. The old pistol he had was one shot away from blowin' up in his face.'

'I do not believe you, *gringo*. The old man was found lying not far from the wagon. He was shot many times.'

'Jesus,' Gabriel said. 'Miguel's dead?' His blood went cold. 'What about the woman? She dead, too?'

'Only you know that,' Captain

Morales snapped. 'I ask you again — where is she? What have you done with her?'

'Nothin'. I already told you that, goddammit. Last time I saw her she was — '

'Was it her gold you were after?' Captain Morales held up a US gold eagle.

'Where'd you get that?'

'It was on the ground where you dropped it after robbing her.'

'Robb — ? Hell, I didn't even know she had any gold.'

'Why else would you kill them?'

'I *didn't* kill them.'

'How much more gold was there?' Captain Morales demanded. 'And where did you hide it? Tell me and it will go better for you.'

'Mean won't hang me twice?'

'*Gringo*, it is not wise to mock me.'

'Then quit accusin' me of somethin' I didn't do, for Chrissake! I liked that old man an' I liked the woman too. But even if I hadn't, there was no reason for me to shoot them.'

'But you cannot deny they were at your *rancho*. I saw their wagon tracks there with my own eyes.'

'Who's denyin' it?'

'This makes you the last person to see them alive.'

'Not the last. That'd be the *hombre* who pulled the trigger.'

Gabriel saw the officer didn't believe him.

'Look, *Capitán*,' he said, trying to control his anger, 'I know it looks suspicious. And I understand why you think I killed them. But I didn't, so help me God I didn't. The last time I saw Ellie an' the old man, they were alive. We said goodbye an' they headed back this way.'

'When was that?'

'Early mornin', day before yesterday. They'd spent the night at my place. I even gave them food and water to take with them. Does that sound like someone plannin' to shoot them later?'

'A man with gold on his mind will do

anything to get it,' said Captain Morales. 'You will either tell me where it is, and what you have done with the señorita, or I will whip it out of you. And then I will hang you.'

'For what? You got no proof I shot anyone.'

'That is where you are wrong, *gringo*. *El director de pompas fúnebres* is burying the proof at this very moment.' He walked off, slamming the jail door behind him before Gabriel could repeat that he hadn't shot Escalero.

14

Alone, Gabriel lay on the bunk wondering if Ellie was still alive. And if she was, who had kidnapped her.

The obvious answer was *bandidos de montana,* as the locals called the renegades who roamed the Sierras. They had probably ambushed the wagon, gunned down Escalero when he tried to defend Ellen, found the gold and ridden off with her. But to where? And what did they intend to do with her? Torture her? Pass her around among each other? Give her to their whores for amusement? Sell her to other bandits? The possibilities were endless. And what would happen to her once everyone grew tired of her?

The answer to that chilled Gabriel's blood. He sat up, his mind suddenly clear. He had to break out, track down the bandits and find a way to rescue

Ellie. And he had to do it fast!

He clamped his hat over his face to protect it from the flies, closed his eyes and began thinking of how he could escape.

No one bothered Gabriel all day. He had expected to be interrogated again by Captain Morales, but afternoon turned into evening and the pompous, strutting little officer never showed. Neither did the jailor with food or water. Gabriel realized then that Morales was more interested in the gold than hanging him, and intended to force him into revealing its whereabouts by starving him.

Well, he thought wryly, why not give the man what he wants?

★　★　★

Dawn arrived. Since the cell had no windows Gabriel had to guess what time it was by the sound of the jailor stirring in the outer office. By now he had a raging thirst and could have eaten two of his own ham-eggs-and-biscuits breakfasts.

Presently the door opened and Captain Morales strutted in. Gabriel had to hand it to him. Despite the heat and the early hour he looked as immaculate in his fancy uniform as any parade officer!

Behind him slouched the jailor, carrying a small table and a chair. He placed them before Gabriel's cell, withdrew then reappeared shortly with a bowl of fruit, two cups, pot of coffee and a pitcher of water. He set them on the table, saluted Captain Morales and left, locking the door behind him.

The officer sat at the table and smiled at Gabriel. 'I thought perhaps you would enjoy sharing my breakfast,' he said affably.

'Nothin' I'd like better.'

'First, you must share something with me.'

'I'm way ahead of you, *Capitán*. The gold's hidden in my cabin.'

Captain Morales gave a wolfish smile.

'It is not good to start a confession with a lie, *gringo*. My men have already searched what is left of your cabin. The gold is not there.'

'Oh, it's there all right. You just didn't look in the right place.'

The officer studied him, not sure if he should believe him.

'If you'll take me there, *Capitán*, I'll show you where it is.'

'And if you are lying, *gringo?*'

'Shoot me.' Gabriel grinned. 'It'll save you the price of a hangin'.'

15

Hands tied to his saddle horn, Gabriel rode alongside Captain Morales at the head of the tiny column. The stallion, as if sensing the gravity of the situation, had made no attempt to act up during the entire ride. But now, as they crested a steep rocky rise and saw the vast desert valley spread out before them, the Morgan pricked its ears and, anxious to be turned loose, quickened its stride.

Captain Morales kicked up his horse, making it keep abreast of the stallion.

'Do not do anything stupid,' he warned Gabriel. 'My men have strict orders to shoot you if you try to escape.'

'Don't boil your brains,' Gabriel advised him. 'I ain't goin' anywhere.'

It took them another thirty minutes to cross the flat, barren valley and reach the *rancho*. Captain Morales ordered his men to dismount and surround the blackened shell of the cabin. Despite the long ride and intense heat they obeyed at the double, sombreros flopping, spurs jingling, rifles held at the ready.

Captain Morales then pressed his pistol against Gabriel's back, ordered him to walk slowly, and together they entered the ruins.

'Before I give you the gold,' Gabriel said, pausing amid the ashes, 'do I have your word you won't shoot me?'

'As an officer and a *caballero*, I swear it so,' Captain Morales said. 'Now, where is the gold?'

'Under here.' Gabriel indicated the charred remains of the clothes' chest. 'Buried in the dirt.'

Captain Morales kept the pistol trained on Gabriel and ordered him to dig up the gold.

'I'll need your saber.'

Keeping his pistol trained on Gabriel, the officer drew his sword and stuck it in the ground.

Gabriel scraped the ashes aside and

began to dig. When he was a foot or so down, he uncovered a rusty metal box.

'Help yourself, *Capitán*.'

'Lift it out.'

Gabriel obeyed and opened the lid to reveal a canvas sack on which lay coiled a — rattlesnake.

'Don't worry,' he said as the alarmed officer jumped back. 'It's dead. See,' he slipped the point of the saber under the snake, lifted it up and in the same motion flung it at Captain Morales.

The dead snake wrapped around the officer's face. He stumbled back with a cry. Gabriel jumped him. Slugging Morales with the handle of the sword, he grabbed the pistol and pressed it against the captain's temple.

'Tell your men to drop their rifles an' wait for you down at the creek. Do it, goddammit,' he hissed when the officer hesitated, 'or I swear to sweet Jesus I'll put a hole through your brain.'

Captain Morales grudgingly obeyed.

Gabriel waited until the six unarmed *Rurales* were lined up in the hot sun like toy soldiers. Then he let Morales up and told him to join his men. The officer obeyed without uttering a word.

Gabriel then opened the sack and took out a well-worn gun belt, which was wrapped around a holster containing a Colt .45. He strapped it on, fastened the tie-down around his thigh, pocketed a box of cartridges and carried the sack outside to the stallion. He tucked it under his bedroll, mounted up and rode to the crest of the slope.

'There is no gold,' he shouted to Captain Morales. 'Never was. That gold eagle you found, it must've belonged to the shooter.'

'It is of no importance,' Captain Morales replied. 'I shall hang you anyway.'

'We'll argue about that later,' Gabriel said. 'Right now I'm goin' after the woman. An' if you or any of your yahoos try to follow me, I'll dry-gulch every last one of you.'

He kicked the stallion into an easy lope and rode off toward the distant mountains.

16

That evening he made camp high in the rocky foothills. Towering above him the mountain peaks formed a jagged skyline. An eagle swept effortlessly over the treetops, its single cry soon lost in the vast silent emptiness.

Gabriel removed the saddle and bedroll from the stallion's back, and left the Morgan untied so it could defend itself against any marauding mountain lions.

A bitter wind off the Sierras kept him shivering. But not wanting to attract bandits, he decided against lighting a fire. There were a few strips of jerky in his saddlebag; he chewed one of them, making each bite last as long as he could. But he couldn't fool his belly and it grumbled for hot beans and coffee. Consoling himself with the thought that tomorrow he might get lucky and shoot a rabbit or a deer, he stretched out on his bedroll, rifle next to him, and lit a cigar.

As he smoked, to keep his mind off Ellie he idly toyed with his Peacemaker, spinning the cylinder and twirling the heavy single-action Colt around on his forefinger. The .45 had fancy ebony grips which were worn smooth from constant use, so smooth he could barely make out the initials M. J. engraved on them.

Mesquite Jennings, he thought wryly. How the hell did he ever come up with a dime-novel name like that? He chuckled, more from disgust than amusement, and tucked the gun back in its holster. After crossing the border and isolating himself in the cabin, he'd never expected to use it again. He'd also felt that by burying the gun he was burying his past. But, as he had learned so often over the years, gunmen with a price on their head seldom got to bury their past or choose their own future.

Resting his head on his saddle, he

gazed up at the dark clouds that were gathering overhead. Luck was with him, he realized. Without a moon, anyone passing would not see him hidden among the rocks.

Somewhere, far off, a mountain lion screamed.

It was the last thing he remembered before falling asleep.

★   ★   ★

He woke up before dawn broke. A dense white mist had descended from the mountains, shrouding everything. Its cold dampness made him shiver. Still huddled under his blanket he listened for a moment, trying to pick up any threatening sound. All he heard was silence. He pulled on his boots, stamped a few times to get his blood going, then relieved himself behind a rock before saddling the stallion.

Oh, Lord, what he wouldn't do for a cup of hot coffee!

He tied his bedroll behind the saddle

and went to put his boot in the stirrup. But the horse suddenly shied away and Gabriel went sprawling. Cursing, he slapped the stallion on the rump until it backed up in between two rocks. Then he tried again. The Morgan twitched a few times and cow-kicked, but made no attempt to buck him off.

'I'm probably givin' you too much credit,' Gabriel told it, 'but if that was payback for me whackin' you with the rifle, we're even now. So don't give me any more crap.'

Pissed off because of the way the day had begun, he cut his last cigar in half, lit it and tried to enjoy it as he rode up into the mountains.

Usually, the higher the elevation the thicker the mist. Today the world was upside down and after a few hours he broke through the mist and found himself following a narrow trail that curved sharply up between dense patches of green shrubs and bushes. Ahead, much higher, dense oak and pine forests clung precariously to the increasingly steep rocky slopes.

He craned his neck and looked up at the rugged peaks that surrounded him on all sides. Silhouetted against the pale blue sky they looked so wild and majestic that normally they would have taken his breath away. But today his mind was on Ellie, and how he must find her quickly, and the scenery had no effect on him.

The trail climbed ever upward. As if to match it the brilliant sun climbed higher in the sky. Gabriel felt its heat through his hat. He closed his eyes and dozed, trusting the stallion to find the easiest way through the mountains.

He must have fallen asleep in the saddle because the next thing he knew the Morgan stopped so suddenly that he was thrown against its muscular arched neck.

Jolted awake, Gabriel looked over the stallion's head — in time to see a green rat-snake slither across the trail.

'Calm down, you big baby,' he told the jittery horse. 'It ain't gonna bite you.'

The non-venomous constrictor disappeared into the bushes. Gabriel nudged the stallion forward and tried to go back to sleep. It was impossible. The trail had become so steep he had to cling onto the horn just to prevent himself from sliding backward out of the saddle.

They were high up now, and even the invincible Morgan began to labor in the thin air. Gabriel hated to push it beyond its limits, but every second was precious and he spurred the stallion onward.

Shortly after, they rounded a corner and Gabriel saw a large boulder blocking the trail. He grinned as if seeing an old friend. How about that, he thought. After all these years, and he'd found it like it was marked on a map.

He dismounted, and led the horse around the boulder. The trail was covered in loose shale, making it treacherous under foot. Several times the ground suddenly crumbled away causing Gabriel to stumble and almost lose his balance. Ahead, the trail became dangerously narrow in places and the outer edge of the cliff dropped straight down for 1,000 feet.

Gabriel kept his eyes fixed in front of him, leading the nervous stallion along a winding dirt path that cut through giant slab-sided rocks before disappearing into a wooded *barranca*.

Pausing at the mouth of the deep canyon, he stripped off his shirt and swapped it for one he took from the sack. This shirt was white and loose-fitting, like a *poncho*, and hung below his belt. He removed his hat, took out a red cloth and wrapped it around his head. Then he remounted, spurred the stallion forward and rode into the woods.

Soon he smelled burning pine needles. He slowed the horse to a walk. They passed under a large rocky overhang. Ahead, the tree-studded cliffs on either side of him were dotted with caves. Smoke curled out from some of them. And as

Gabriel rode closer he glimpsed a white-clad figure holding a bow and a fistful of arrows, watching him from behind a rock.

Making sure his hands were not near his rifle or six-gun, he rode further into the canyon. Eyes watched him from various caves and rocks. Gabriel ignored them. Shortly, he reached a clear, shallow stream. He dismounted, knelt and drank from it. The stallion waded in and drank greedily. When Gabriel had quenched his thirst he sat hunkered on his heels and smoked the second half of his cigar.

Nothing stirred. High overhead two hawks circled, drifting effortlessly on thermals.

Gabriel waited patiently, slowly smoking the cigar down to the ash. Then he heard a faint movement behind him. He made no move to see who it was. A shadow passed across his face as a Tarahumara Indian shyly joined him. About Gabriel's age but much smaller, he wore a *poncho* shirt hanging over his loose white pants, a red headband and *huarache* sandals. He sat cross-legged beside Gabriel but never once looked at him.

Moments later, two more similarly dressed Raramúri — The Runners as they call themselves — arrived. They didn't look at him either. He ignored them and chewed on his cigar butt.

After a long wait their chief, Victoriano Guitierez, joined them. He was dressed like the others, except he wore a wraparound loin-cloth instead of pants and a colorful beaded belt around his waist. Under a red headband his long black hair was streaked with silver and his brown face was badly crinkled. But his eyes were still beaver-bright and his smile ageless. A lifetime of running up and down mountainsides had kept him lithe and graceful and he walked silently or, as their cousins the Pimas say 'with air under his feet'.

Sitting opposite Gabriel, he said. 'Welcome. It is good to see my White Brother again.'

'You too, Victoriano . . . ' It had been ages since Gabriel had spoken Tarahumara, one of the many dialects of the Uto-Aztecan language, and he hoped he was pronouncing the words correctly.

'We' — Victoriano gestured toward the three-man council — 'have long wondered what it was we said that offended you so badly you stayed away all these years.'

Remembering it was considered impolite to speak too quickly after another had spoken, Gabriel waited a moment before explaining that no one had offended him. On the contrary, he said, the Raramúri had sheltered him when he needed shelter, befriended him when he needed friends, and, above all, treated him with kindness and respect, making him feel like a man again. Pausing to let his words sink in, he then added that the reason he had not returned to see them until now was because for most of those years he had either been in prison or hiding from the law.

Victoriano and the council absorbed Gabriel's words in solemn silence. Presently they nodded to each other as if agreeing to accept his explanation for his long absence.

'We are pleased to hear you say this,' Victoriano said to Gabriel. 'Because to insult a guest, even unintentionally, brings great shame and dishonor to our people.'

Now that the ice had been broken Gabriel and the soft-spoken, reclusive Indians talked about everything from his previous stay with them to how poorly their crops had grown this year. Hunting too had been bad. Their finest trackers and distance runners had only run down six deer since the season of the hot sun began.

When Gabriel enquired whether there was any reason for the lack of game during summer, the council exchanged troubled looks, as if uneasy about answering his question.

'Has my absence been so long,' Gabriel asked them, 'that my brothers can no longer tell me the truth?'

Victoriano spoke for the council. Ever since the Spanish arrived many centuries ago and tried to conquer them, he said, the Raramúri had been driven higher and higher into the *Barranca del Cobre*. But they had always remained free and supported themselves by hunting, farming and cattle rearing. Now, he added angrily, rumors of silver mines had lured hordes of whites and mestizos into the mountains, their need for fresh meat threatening to exterminate all the deer and other wild game.

When Gabriel asked Victoriano what the council planned to do about the invaders, the chief shrugged and replied, what could they do? Unlike the whites, who were more numerous than raindrops, the Raramúri could not afford to start an all-out war. For, regardless of the final outcome, the great loss of young men would make them losers.

'No,' he concluded bitterly, 'war is not the answer for my people. We must avoid conflict at all costs.'

'We shall move our families higher into the mountains,' Luna Chacarito, the youngest council member, put in angrily, 'as high as the Cloud Forests if necessary. For only that way will our women and children be safe from the guns of the whites and mestizos.'

There was a long silence. Gabriel hoped he wasn't looking at a people facing extinction. He also hoped he could find a way to mention why he was there without offending them or making it seem like he was only there for his own benefit. The Raramúri were a generous, sensitive, giving people and expected little in return. But they were not stupid and knew when they were being used.

As if reading his mind, Victoriano said: 'Enough about our pain. Why has my White Brother chosen this day to return to us?'

'I need your help,' Gabriel replied. He then explained about Ellen being kidnapped by bandits, adding that eventually he could track them down and perhaps find a way to rescue her. But this would take time, lots of time, and by then the woman might be dead or worse. But if he could use one of their expert trackers, he'd find her quickly and maybe still save her life.

Victoriano and the council nodded to show they understood his urgency, but no one spoke. Sensing they wanted to discuss the matter alone, Gabriel excused himself and sat on a rock while the Indians talked.

Above him, now that he'd been accepted, women in bright-colored sacklike tunics and long woolen skirts emerged from the caves with their children in tow. Gabriel recognized some of them and waved. They shyly acknowledged him and went about their daily chores.

Time dragged by. The Rarámuri were a deliberate people and Gabriel knew better than to try to rush them.

At last the council discussion ended and Victoriano joined him. It was decided, he said. Their best tracker,

Cerrildo, would go with Gabriel to help him find his woman. But before this could happen everyone had to participate in a special *tesguinada*. At the religious ceremony the men would consume large quantities of an extra-strong *sugiki*, allowing their spirits to roam free so they could persuade their God to look favorably upon Gabriel's search.

Gabriel, who'd often gotten cockeyed drunk on maize beer when he'd stayed here before, wished he could start searching for Ellen at once. But there was no chance of that, not if he wanted Cerrildo to track for him. *Tesguino*, he knew, was as important to the Raramúri culture as astronomy was to the Mayans. So he unsaddled the stallion, left it loose, and accompanied Victoriano and the council up the steep rocky slope to the main cave.

17

The ceremonial drinking and dancing lasted until darkness. By then Victoriano's wish had become true: most of the adults were falling-down drunk.

Gabriel wasn't in much better shape. Bleary-eyed, he sat sprawled against a rock, numbly trying to focus on the shadowy figures stumbling around the blazing fire.

Presently one approached him. As the man's round brown face swam into view, Gabriel realized it was the young tracker, Cerrildo.

'Can you walk?' he asked, prodding Gabriel with his bow.

Gabriel nodded and staggered to his feet. It was a struggle to pick up his saddle, but he eventually managed it and followed Cerrildo down the treacherously steep path that led to the base of the cliff.

He could have used a helping hand, but knew Cerrildo would consider it an insult to help him; so, slipping and stumbling, he kept going and somehow made it safely to the bottom. Here, he suffered a dizzy spell, preventing him from walking, and eventually had to throw up in the bushes before he could continue.

Cerrildo watched him in stoic amusement, waiting patiently while Gabriel groggily saddled up and got mounted. Then, at a dog-trot, the Indian led the way out of the canyon.

★ ★ ★

Except for two occasions when Gabriel had to stop to vomit, the threesome descended at the same effortless pace for about four hours. They were now on the lower slopes of the mountain and could see the shadowy peaks of the foothills below them in the distance.

During a pause Cerrildo told Gabriel that bandits rarely camped at the higher altitudes, but from here on they might run into them. He then asked Gabriel to wait while he checked the trail ahead, then vanished into the darkness.

Knowing that the Raramúri hunted deer by running them into exhaustion then slitting their throats, Gabriel crooked one leg over the saddle horn and prepared for a long wait.

The Morgan stirred restlessly under him and Gabriel sensed the horse was getting ready to buck him off.

'You do,' he warned, as if the stallion could understand him, 'an' so help me Hannah I'll shoot you right between the ears.'

A half-hour passed. Then Cerrildo suddenly reappeared out of the brush. He could see a campfire in the hills several miles ahead, he said. Bandits? Gabriel asked him. Cerrildo shrugged and said it could be bandits, whites or mestizos. The only way to be sure was to get closer. Was his White Brother well enough to continue? Gabriel, who felt he had nothing left to throw up, nodded grimly and kicked the stallion into a nice easy lope.

The camp belonged to a party of white prospectors, veterans who had dug for gold and silver from Colorado to California to Mexico. Most of them were asleep in their tents, but a few sat passing a jug around the fire.

There was no sign of women, but Gabriel insisted on making sure Ellen wasn't tied up in one of the tents before leaving. Sober now, though still queasy, he followed Cerrildo quietly through the brush to the edge of the camp. Then, unseen, they crept from tent to tent, peering under each flap until Gabriel was satisfied Ellen wasn't a prisoner.

As they withdrew he felt a sense of moral obligation to his Indian friends. Once he and Cerrildo were safely out of the camp he suggested they try to drive the usurpers from the mountains.

Cerrildo beamed. He'd seen the carcasses of two deer hanging in the camp and at once thought of the hunger his people were enduring because of the prospectors. So, after wrapping grass around the shafts of two of his arrows, he set fire to them and shot them into the nearest tents.

The fire quickly spread to the other tents, driving out the men sleeping inside. In moments the camp was in an uproar. Gabriel helped increase the panic by firing shots above the prospectors' heads.

There were only a dozen men, he thought, as he and Cerrildo watched the prospectors fleeing. But what the hell, it was a start.

Disappointed that he hadn't found Ellen, Gabriel rode through the night behind the tireless Indian.

By dawn they had cleared the mountains and from a hilltop trail could see the desert sprawled out below them. It changed colors as the rising sun slowly traveled across the sky, turning into a vast pastel emptiness that stretched to the distant horizon.

When the sun was directly overhead,

signaling noon, they found shade under a rocky overhang. Sweating, Gabriel poured water from his canteen into the crown of his campaign hat and let the stallion drink. Then, while it fed on nearby shrubs, he and Cerrildo quenched their thirst and ate a handful of dried maize. When they were finished they moved on, deeper into the hills.

The day passed without any sign of bandits. The sun slid below the rugged skyline. Dusk arrived and with it swarms of mosquitoes. Gabriel's frustration mounted. If they didn't find Ellen soon, the bandits might tire of her and . . .

Ahead, Cerrildo motioned for Gabriel to stop, and knelt down to examine the trail.

Gabriel's pulse quickened. No slouch as a tracker himself, he saw nothing in the sandy dirt and dismounted to get a closer look. But Cerrildo waved him back and held up both hands followed by one finger. Gabriel nodded to show he understood that eleven riders had passed this way.

'Bandits?' he mouthed. Cerrildo nodded. Gabriel then mimed: 'which way?' and the tracker pointed down the hill to his left, indicating a wooded canyon below them.

Even as Gabriel looked smoke spiraled up from the treetops. At the same time he heard raucous laughter.

'The woman,' he whispered, 'is she with them?'

The Indian shrugged. Waving Gabriel closer, he pointed at one set of tracks. Hunkering down, Gabriel noticed the imprints were slightly deeper than the others and nodded to show he understood: this horse carried extra weight, possibly two riders — one of which might be Ellen.

18

They followed the winding trail down through the dense brush into the canyon. Luck seemed to be with them. The bandits apparently felt safe enough not to post sentries and Gabriel and Cerrildo got within thirty yards of the camp without being detected. The Indian then indicated that they should go the rest of the way on foot.

Gabriel dismounted, tied the Morgan to a bush — something it didn't like — collected his Winchester and followed Cerrildo through the trees.

It was almost dark now. Beyond the low bushes ahead of them Gabriel could see a row of tethered horses. His gaze shifted and he spotted the bandits gathered around a fire. All ages, most of them were swilling tequila and their conversation was constantly interrupted by loud, drunken laughter. Behind them was a wall of rock on which their shadows, distorted by the firelight, danced grotesquely.

Gabriel and Cerrildo closed in, close enough now to distinguish the bandits' faces. Most were bearded, shabbily dressed and poorly armed. Many didn't even have boots.

But there was no sign of Ellen.

Frustrated, Gabriel was about to suggest they pull back when he heard a scream. It was a woman's scream and as Gabriel and Cerrildo looked, three bandits dragged someone out from behind the horses. The captive kicked and struggled to break loose. Her outer garments were badly torn, she was barefoot and there were scratches on her arms and legs.

Gabriel couldn't see her face, but he knew by the shortness of her pale hair that it was Ellen!

Rage flared through him. Forgetting caution, he was about to open fire on the bandits when Cerrildo pulled his rifle down.

Indicating his bow, the Indian mimed for Gabriel to let him shoot a few bandits first, lessening the odds, and then start firing.

Calming, Gabriel nodded.

Cerrildo drew an arrow back, aimed and loosed the shaft. A man at the fire silently fell forward. A second followed before anyone realized the first was dead. Cerrildo went to shoot again but at that moment, behind them, the stallion mistook a fallen branch for a snake. Panicking, it reared up, neighing shrilly.

The bandits whirled around, grabbing up their weapons. Any chance of surprise was gone.

Silently cursing the Morgan, Gabriel opened fire at the bandits holding Ellen. Two went down. But the third was smart enough to pull her in front of him like a shield forcing Gabriel to hold his fire.

He watched helplessly as the man dragged her behind a rock.

On the other side of the fire the row

of panicked horses broke loose from the tie-line and scattered in all directions.

Meanwhile, Cerrildo's arrows brought down two more bandits. But the remainder took cover, firing wildly into the brush.

'Here,' Gabriel tossed his rifle to Cerrildo. 'Keep 'em pinned down.' Ducking low, he ran through the brush toward Ellen.

Cerrildo fired until the Winchester was empty. He then dropped it and quickly started shooting arrows at the four bandits.

★ ★ ★

The bandit holding Ellen was facing Cerrildo and didn't see Gabriel coming until the last moment. He desperately swung his pistol around to shoot, but he was too late. Gabriel had already fired. The .45 slug slammed into the bandit's chest, sending him stumbling backward.

Gabriel grabbed Ellen and pulled her

down behind the rock. About to ask her if she was all right, he saw by her vacant stare that she was in shock. He gently put his arm around her. She cringed and didn't seem to recognize him.

'Ellie . . . Ellie, it's me, Gabe . . . '

For a second she didn't respond. Then recognition replaced the terror in her eyes and she moved her lips, murmuring something he couldn't hear.

Reassuring her with a smile, he told her to keep down, and peered over the rock in time to see the last three bandits rushing at Cerrildo.

Out of arrows, the slender Indian knocked the first bandit down with a swipe of his bow, then drew his knife and leaped at the other two.

Gabe shot one of them in the neck, dropping him instantly. He then shot the first bandit, just as the fallen man started to get up.

Meanwhile, Cerrildo and the last bandit grappled on the ground. A shot rang out. Cerrildo stiffened then plunged his knife in the bandit's chest. The Mexican died trying to pull it out.

Grasping Ellen's hand, Gabriel led her over to Cerrildo. The Indian was gut-shot and sat there holding his belly, blood seeping through his fingers.

Gabriel gently pried his hands aside, took one look at the wound and knew it was over.

Cerrildo knew it, too. He smiled as he saw Ellen was safe and nodded as if satisfied. Then he leaned back against a rock and silently prayed to his God.

He was dead within moments.

Gabriel, surprised by how quickly he'd died from a belly wound, sadly closed Cerrildo's eyelids. It was then that he noticed the blood on the Indian's shirt, and realized he'd also been shot in the chest.

Moved by Cerrildo's courage, and at the same time enraged by the injustice of it all, Gabriel picked up the body and carried it to a small clearing among the trees.

Ellen came with him, less fearful now

that the fighting had stopped. She watched silently as Gabriel dug a shallow grave with his knife, placed the body in it and then covered it with dirt and rocks.

'Be fittin' if you spoke over him,' he told her.

She hesitated, as if not understanding him.

'Never mind,' Gabriel said. 'I'll do it.'

'No,' she said, the first audible words she'd actually spoken. 'He died because of me. I must pray for him.' Kneeling, she clasped her hands together and prayed over the grave.

When she was finished Gabriel helped her up. Together they started back along the trail. He started to ask her if she was all right, but she cut him off and told him not to question her about what happened. She did not want to talk about it. Tears filled her eyes as she spoke, and he didn't press her further.

A little later they came upon the Morgan. It stood near the bush it had been tied to, a broken branch still caught in the dangling reins.

Gabriel felt like shooting it. The stallion seemed to sense it had done something wrong. Trembling, it made no effort to bite or shy away as Gabriel took his shirt from the saddlebag and gave it to Ellen. Before she would put it on, she asked him for water. He gave her his canteen but instead of drinking, she poured water on her legs and groin and washed the blood away.

'Why are you angry with him?' she asked Gabriel as she buttoned on the shirt. When he explained that if the horse hadn't neighed, he and Cerrildo would probably have killed all the bandits without either of them getting shot, Ellen disagreed.

'It was his time to join God,' she said simply. 'Nothing could change that.'

'If that's true, how do you know it's not Brandy's time, too?' Drawing his Colt, Gabriel held it against the Morgan's head. 'All it would take is a twitch of my finger.'

'Because that wouldn't be a random bullet,' she said. 'Besides, hasn't there been enough killing?'

He knew she was right. He holstered his gun, untied his blanket and wrapped it around Ellen, saying it would lessen the chafing. He then stepped into the saddle, pulled her up behind him and dug his spurs into the stallion.

19

With Ellen clinging tightly to him, they rode out of the hills in silence, following the trail as it sloped gently down into the desert. Clouds covered the moon and Gabriel decided it was dark enough to make camp for the night. Ahead, several large boulders formed a half-circle, offering them shelter from the wind. Gabriel dismounted close to the largest rock and helped Ellen down. Then he unsaddled the Morgan and turned it loose. It ran off into the darkness as if ashamed of itself.

'Aren't you afraid he won't come back?' Ellen asked as Gabriel spread out his bedroll for her.

'My luck ain't that good,' he said, only half-joking.

She looked at him and shook her head. 'You're a strange man, Gabriel Moonlight.'

'Why? 'Cause I'm not in love with my horse?'

'I — I'm not saying you have to love him. But surely it would be helpful if you liked him. I mean, you spend so much time together.'

'A cowboy an' his faithful pony . . . roamin' the land together . . . partners to the end . . . that kinda thing?'

'Well, yes, I — '

'Responsible for each other's well-bein'?'

'Exactly.'

He gave a disgusted snort.

'Eyewash.'

'I beg your pardon?'

'That's Easterners talkin'. Only thing they know 'bout the West is what they read. Book-writers, now they're paid to keep the dream goin'. Always paint pretty pictures when they write about a cowboy an' his pony. Give the horses romantic names like Ol' Brown or Sandy or Paint, an' call the men Shorty or Smokey or Sugarfoot — make it seem like they all get up and kiss every mornin'.'

'You don't have to be sarcastic — '

'Truth is,' Gabriel continued, 'most trail hands I ever mixed with would've traded their horse for the price of a thick steak.'

'Oh, I don't believe that. Not for a second.'

'Been on many cattle drives, have you?'

'N-No, of course I haven't.'

'Mostly, cowboys don't even know which mount they're drawin' from the *remuda* — an' wouldn't give two damns if they did. As for bein' responsible,' he added, 'that's only true regardin' stable horses. They've been sugar-treated an' need lookin' after. Brandy, now, he may look like he belongs in a stall but that ain't his mentality. He can carry his own water an' neither of us would have it any other way.'

She'd never realized he could be so rude or cynical.

'If you dislike him so much, why don't you sell him and buy another?'

''Cause I'm not stupid. Brandy's the finest horse I'll ever own. An' I'd have to have salt for brains to get rid of him. 'Sides, you don't have to like somethin' to know its worth, Ellie. You just have to respect it. That's enough.' He knew he was being rude, even mean-spirited, but he couldn't help himself: he had to somehow rid himself of the anger he felt over losing Cerrildo.

As if to make up for it, he made a pillow out of his saddle for her, and gave her a handful of dried maize.

'Munch on this and then drink a little water. It'll take the bite off your hunger.'

'Dare we light a fire? I'm f-freezing.'

'A small one, maybe.' He drew his Colt, thumbed the cylinder so that there was a cartridge under the hammer and offered it to her.

She shrank back. 'No, I don't want it.'

'Suit yourself. But remember, a gun saved your life tonight.' He strode off into the darkness before she could say anything.

Alone, Ellen felt all her fears

returning. She regretted not going with Gabriel and sat there straining to hear the slightest noise. Her flesh crawled. She could still feel the bandits' hands pawing at her, tearing away her clothes, and throwing her to the ground; feel the weight of their bodies; hear their drunken laughter; smell their foul breath lingering in her nostrils.

'Oh God,' she sobbed. 'Dear God, why did you forsake me?' He did not forsake you, her conscience reminded her. It was you who chose to forsake him. You reneged on your vow to serve him in order to seek revenge, to take up the sword against three of his children. Is it any wonder you are being punished?

A noise startled her, and she had to fight not to cry out.

But it was only the stallion, blacker than the night, standing in front of her. Its eyes glinted in the darkness. It watched her for a few moments, as if trying to understand what she was doing. Then it lowered its head and pushed its velvety soft nose against her cheek.

There was something wonderfully comforting in its touch and Ellen held the nose close to her, wetting it with her tears.

At last the Morgan snuffled softly, then pulled back, tossed its head and melted into the night.

* * *

Backs to the darkness the two of them sat by the crackling fire, warming their hands and watching the flickering flames vanish into thin air like the fingers of a ghostly shaman.

For a long time they didn't talk, content to just sit there, close together, minds churning, wind moaning in their ears.

Then, 'Thank you,' she whispered suddenly.

'Don't heap credit on me,' Gabriel said. 'Cerrildo, he's the one who deserves it. Without him I'd still be combing the hills for you.'

'I didn't mean for rescuing me — I'll never be able to thank you enough for that, you or Cerrildo. I meant for not making me ride one of their horses.'

He frowned at her. 'Thought you weren't gonna talk about that?'

'I'm not.' She shivered, but from recent memories, not the cold. 'They killed Miguel, you know. Shot your pistol out of his hand, threw a rope over him and pulled him off the wagon. Then one of them dragged him around behind his horse while the others shot him, kept shooting him, shooting and laughing, even after he was dead — '

He stopped her and pulled her close. 'Torturin' yourself isn't the answer.'

'I know. And I don't want to talk about it. Or even think about it. Ever. But, you see, I have to. Awful as it was, I just have to. If I don't, I'll explode.'

'Then at least get some rest first. In the mornin', while we're ridin', if you still feel like it, you can tell me all about it.'

'Yes,' she said distantly, 'in the morning. I'll feel better then.'

For a few moments she was silent, her gaze fixed on the flames, then she blurted: 'After they killed Miguel, I thought they were going to shoot me too. So I offered them the gold. I know I shouldn't have,' she said seeing Gabriel's frown. 'I mean, I know you told me not to tell anyone I had any gold but, well, I was so frightened that I . . . I thought perhaps if I gave it to them they'd be so happy and grateful they'd let me go. But of course they didn't. They, the one, the leader I mean, forced me to mount up behind him and then he and the rest of them, we all rode up into the hills and . . . Oh God, dear God,' she said covering her face with her hands, 'you're right, I mustn't talk about this, I must try to forget it, to pretend that it never happened . . . but of course I can't, I never will . . . never ever . . . ' She broke off, sobbing.

★ ★ ★

He held her in his arms all night. The rage he felt for the bandits, for what they had done to Ellen and Cerrildo, kept him warm long after the fire died.

It also made him realize what he had to do next.

And strangely, once he knew, saw it clearly and accepted it, realizing at the same time that fate had planned this outcome all along for him, his rage left him and he lost all fear of hanging.

20

The following dawn, while it was still cool and the heavens ablaze with color, they ate the last of the maize, took a few sips of water, and rode slowly toward San Dimas.

Knowing he was risking his neck if he ran into the *Rurales*, Gabriel considered skirting the sleepy pueblo and taking their chances with the desert: a sixty-mile stretch of burning desolation that had to be crossed in order to reach the American border. Like the desert south-west of San Dimas it too was known as *Viaje del Muerto*. Thinking about it Gabriel doubted if Ellen could make it all the way across. He doubted if Brandy could either, since even the indomitable Morgan was showing signs of tiring under its double load.

No, he thought resignedly, it had to be San Dimas.

They rode on, now able to see the familiar church bell tower above the whitewashed adobe buildings in the distance.

It was time, Gabriel realized, to tell Ellen about the potential trouble that lay ahead. Keeping his tone casual so as not to alarm her, he explained about his run-in with Captain Morales.

She fooled him; as if accustomed to confrontations with the law, she calmly assured him that he hadn't a thing to worry about. All she had to do was tell Captain Morales that it was bandits who killed Miguel and kidnapped her, and Gabriel would be exonerated.

He wasn't so sure. He knew that he had sorely damaged the captain's *machismo* by knocking him on his ass in front of his men, and guessed the arrogant officer would need to prove he had bigger *cojones* than a renegade *gringo* gunman.

'Nonsense,' Ellen said when Gabriel told her about his problem. 'When I spoke to him he seemed like a most understanding gentleman. I was quite taken with him in fact. I'm sure when he hears the truth — especially after all I've been through — he'll happily overlook your transgressions.'

'I hope you're right,' Gabriel said. ''Cause I don't intend to let that Mexican rooster lock me in the *calabozo* a second time.'

★ ★ ★

San Dimas was too small to keep a secret. Everyone had heard about Gabriel's run-in with the *Rurales* and was surprised to see him ride into town; especially with the *gringo* woman, she of the strange hairless head, who they thought had been killed along with her driver.

'We're drawing quite a crowd,' Ellen said to Gabriel as they were escorted through the streets by an ever-increasing number of curious townspeople.

He nodded grimly. 'So much for slippin' in an' out of here without a fuss.'

Ellen smiled at the upturned brown faces trotting alongside them.

'They probably heard I'd been killed and are surprised to see me alive. Either that or it's my hair. I must look like a scalped monkey to them.'

Crossing the sun-baked plaza, Gabriel reined up in front of the livery stable. The same young hostler was already waiting for them in the doorway, anxious to be a part of this spectacle.

Gabriel dismounted and helped Ellen down. Then he told the hostler to feed and water the Morgan. 'We also need a horse. Know any for sale?'

'Sí, señor. I know of a very fine horse. It belongs to my uncle.'

'I just bet it does,' Gabriel said sourly. 'Well, 'long as it's got four legs, send one of your cousins to get it.' He thumbed at the crowd still gathered outside the stable.

'Sí, señor. It will be here when you return.'

Gabriel led Ellen who, despite the intense heat, still had the blanket wrapped around her, to a little dress shop five doors down on the same side of the dirt street. There he bought her a skirt and blouse and a black, wide-brimmed felt hat that made her look like a Navaho. The entire purchase took only a few minutes and Ellen donned everything quickly while Gabriel stood at the window and watched for any sign of the *Rurales*.

'I need shoes,' she complained as he dragged her back toward the stables. 'My feet are one big blister.'

'I'll try to find you some sandals,' he promised. 'But right now you have to get some food in your belly.'

'So do you.'

He nodded and pointed to The Owl cantina across the street. 'You go ahead. Order whatever you like and me the same. I'll join you soon as I take stock of the horse.'

The searing heat had taken its toll on the villagers. The crowd had dwindled and now as Gabriel approached the livery stable, there were only a few curious onlookers gathered outside.

The hostler was waiting for him just inside the doorway with a long-legged blue roan. Gabriel examined it suspiciously.

'Where'd your uncle get a quality horse like this, *amigo?*'

The youthful hostler shrugged his scrawny shoulders.

'I do not know, *señor*. Though this man is my uncle, he is from my father's side of the family, a side I am not so friendly with, and he is like a stranger to me.'

'Well, he knows his horseflesh. This mare looks like she could run all day and night.'

'This is true,' the hostler said solemnly. 'My uncle has told me of this many times. On those occasions when we had reason to talk,' he added, catching himself.

Gabriel didn't believe the youth for a second. But he needed a horse, a good horse, and he needed it fast. And by the way the hostler kept fidgeting and glancing uneasily out the door, he sensed the hostler was in as much of a hurry to close the deal as he was.

'Two hundred pesos,' Gabriel said. 'But you gotta throw in a saddle and bridle.' He knew he was stealing the roan, but he sensed the mare was stolen in the first place and doubted if the hostler would put up much of a fight.

'You are the trader of all traders,' the hostler grumbled.

'Save the gravy for mashed potatoes,' Gabriel said, cutting him off. 'Is it a deal or not?'

'It is, señor. See, I have a fine saddle and bridle hanging in the back there.'

Gabriel could see the saddle and bridle were well-worn but in good shape. He nodded, paid the hostler the money and told him to get the mare saddled while he ate across the street.

He and Ellen were back in ten minutes, still wadding bean-soaked tortillas in their mouths as they entered. The hostler had both horses ready for them. Gabriel mounted quickly and nudged the Morgan out of the stable, into the hot sunlight. Ellen, astride the mare, trotted capably behind him.

'What's her name?' Ellen asked as they cantered through the little town.

'Whatever you want it to be,' Gabriel replied. 'I forgot to ask.'

'Then I'll call her Moonlight, after you. Don't you think it suits her?'

He looked at the mare with its cropped black mane, flowing black tail and silvery-bluish coat, and nodded.

'Grampa Tate's going to love her,' Ellen said, thinking aloud. 'And of course he'll pay you back whatever she cost.'

'Call it a gift, Ellie. I as good as stole her.'

They were approaching the outskirts of the pueblo. Gabriel felt a weight lift from his shoulders. Now all they had to do was make it safely to the border and . . .

Ahead, Captain Morales and his men rode out of a cross-street and blocked their path.

'*Parare!*' the officer barked at him. Then as Gabriel and Ellen reined up: 'You are a bigger fool than I thought, *gringo*. Now I most certainly will hang you.'

'Just a minute, Captain,' Ellen said. 'I'm Ellen Kincaide. And as you can see I am definitely alive.'

'*Silencio, señorita!* This is not of your concern.'

'It most certainly is, sir. If I'm not dead, that means Señor Moonlight cannot be responsible for murdering me ... or my driver. Therefore you have no reason to arrest him.'

Captain Morales wrinkled his thin lips back in a wolfish smile.

'You are mistaken, *señorita*. Assaulting an officer and resisting arrest — both are most serious offenses.'

'But not hangin' offenses,' Gabriel reminded, hand poised over his six-gun.

'No, *gringo*. But horse-stealing is.'

'Horse-stealin'? If you mean the roan, I didn't steal her. I bought her from the hostler.'

'He's telling you the truth,' put in Ellen. 'You can ask the young man. He'll tell you.'

'What he tells me or what you say is of no interest to me,' Captain Morales said smugly. 'This mare is government property. It belongs to Lieutenant Rodriguez. He reported it stolen less than an hour ago. If you doubt me,' he added, 'perhaps you can explain what his initials are doing on your saddle.'

He was talking to Ellen, who now looked down and in front of her left knee saw J. C. R. embossed in the leather.

'This makes you a horse-thief,' Captain Morales said to Gabriel. 'And it will be my pleasure to stretch your neck.' He signaled to his men. 'Take him!'

Gabriel drew his six-gun, so fast it was already in his hand and aimed at Captain Morales' belly before his men could spur their horses forward.

'I don't want to kill you,' he told the officer. 'But if your men make even the slightest move toward me, your next breath will be your last.'

Captain Morales, to his credit, showed no sign of fear.

'After I am dead,' he told his men, 'hang them both.'

21

'Pay no attention to him,' Ellen told Gabriel. 'He's bluffing.'

Gabriel looked at Captain Morales and knew better. The Mexican officer might look like a toy soldier but under his fancy uniform beat a fearless heart.

If they were going to escape, Gabriel knew he had to make his move now.

'Reckon it's time to fold 'em,' he said glumly. Spinning the Peacemaker on his finger, he offered it butt first to Captain Morales. At the same instant he dug his spurs cruelly into the Morgan's flanks, causing the startled horse to rear up.

As it did Gabriel spun the Colt in reverse, grasped the butt and fired alongside the stallion's neck.

The bullet knocked Captain Morales out of the saddle. His mount jumped sideways, crablike, and slammed into the other horses, causing them to panic.

Neighing shrilly, they reared up forcing their riders to hang on with both hands.

By now the Morgan was back on its feet, snorting with anger. Gabriel gripped tightly with his knees and emptied his Colt into the helpless *Rurales*. He deliberately shot high knowing a man could recover from a broken shoulder, and as the way ahead of him cleared he reached back, grasped the roan's bridle and spurred the stallion forward.

'Ride, Ellie! Ride!'

Enraged by the pain of Gabriel's spurs, the stallion charged forward like a battering ram, scattering the soldiers' horses.

The leggy blue roan gamely followed the Morgan, both horses running flat out along the narrow dusty street that ran between two rows of adobe houses and ended at the desert.

They rode this way for about a mile across the wasteland before Gabriel looked back and saw that no one was pursuing them. He then reined up,

Ellen doing the same beside him.

'Reckon I've seen the last of Mexico,' he said drily.

'Gabe, I'm so sorry — '

'Don't be. Nobody twisted my arm to help you.'

'No, but I feel responsible. If I hadn't come here — '

'Forget it, I said.'

He spoke sharply. Ellen shrugged and let it drop.

They rode on, side by side, across the arid, monotonous, unchanging scrubland.

Presently, he said: 'I ever tell you my pa was a circuit rider?'

'H-He was?'

'Colorado, mostly. Went from one gold camp to another, spreadin' God's word to men who prayed on Sunday and spent the rest of the week cuttin' each others' throats over a single nugget.'

'How sad.'

He showed no sign of hearing her.

'Had this sign he carved on a piece of

178

pine. We carried it everywhere with us. An' come meetin' time, Pa made me hang it up in the prayer tent behind him so everyone could read it while he was preachin'.'

He fell silent.

Ellen, seeing how tightly his lips were compressed, his jaw muscles bunched, knew that revealing his past must be hurtful.

Overhead, the sun crawled westward.

'Know what it said?' Gabriel said at last. It said: 'Being a man means being responsible.' He smiled mirthlessly. 'Know where it hangs now? Over the bar in Fat Sally's, biggest whorehouse in Denver.'

'My goodness, how did it end up there?'

'One of the miners at Salt Creek hung it there. A lunger named Cory Doucett. Said that's where it belonged.' Before Ellen could comment, Gabriel added: 'He was drunk when he stole it an' later, when they arrested him, he swore on the Bible, Pa's Bible, that he didn't recall stealin' it or even shootin' off his pistol. But no one believed him, not the judge, jury — not even his own lawyer, he said later.'

'So what happened — did he go to jail?'

'Miners lynched him that same night.'

'For stealing a sign?'

'For shootin' Pa.' He paused and squinted out across the desert. 'George Freely, the miner who slapped the horse out from under him, said afterwards that it wasn't so much about Cory bein' a mean man or evil, though most likely he'd end up in hell anyway, but that, like Pa's sign said, everyone had to be responsible for his own actions.'

* * *

Stopping only for occasional sips of water and to rest the weary horses, they rode slowly across the desert until they reached Cohiba, a collection of adobe hovels inhabited by *campesinos* and their families.

After paying a grubby barefoot boy to look after the horses Gabriel led Ellen to an outdoor cantina. Here, shaded by a tattered awning, they ate double portions of beans, rice and *huevos rancheros*, sopping up the runny egg-yolks with soft tortillas and washing everything down with the local *cerveza*.

They said little. Ellen was especially quiet and had been since Gabriel had told her about his father. Sensing she was still troubled by her ordeal with the bandits, Gabriel left her alone and smoked one of the cheroots he'd bought from the cantina owner.

By the time they had cleaned their plates the entire village was taking a siesta. Bellies stuffed and lethargic from the heat, Gabriel and Ellen fell asleep in their chairs.

Two hours later Gabriel, a light sleeper, was wakened by the faint scraping of a chair. Colt already in his hand, he saw it was Ellen.

'I'll be back in a few minutes,' she promised. Covering her pale wispy hair with her hat, she crossed the plaza and entered the little church.

Wondering how she could find solace in a God that allowed her to be raped and Cerrildo to be cut down in his youth, Gabriel made use of the time by cleaning his Peacemaker. He took the heavy gun apart, blew the sand from the barrel and cylinder then replaced the five, snugly fitting cartridges and put everything together again. This task gave him all the comfort he needed.

Well, maybe not all, he thought thinking of Ellen, but enough. Guns were something a man could rely on. Kept clean and well-oiled, they protected you and never let you down.

Now, as he slid the revolver back into the oiled, worn-smooth holster, he saw Ellie crossing the plaza toward him. Just seeing her lifted his spirits. In her dust-caked Navaho hat, mismatched clothes and with her bare feet tucked into a pair of over-sized *huaraches*, she looked like a misplaced waif. She no longer walked like a spring colt or a young girl hurrying home from school — the bandits had stolen that from her — but she had recovered some of her verve and there was new life in her smile as she waved to him.

'What do you think of my sandals?' she asked, holding up one foot.

'Interesting.'

'Can't you be a little more enthused than that?'

'I was just thinkin',' he said. 'Most folks make donations when they go to church, not walk out with somethin'.'

She laughed. 'I didn't steal them, if that's what you're insinuating. The good padre very kindly gave them to me.'

'Guess he didn't have need of an extra pair.'

'They weren't extra,' Ellen said. 'They were his. I told him I couldn't accept them, but he insisted. Took them right off his feet, God bless him, and put them on mine. That's why they don't fit.'

The priest had apparently given Ellen

something else, Gabriel realized as they rode slowly out of the village: new hope. She appeared more cheerful and chatted endlessly about her childhood at her grandfather's horse ranch. Gabriel listened without interrupting her, quietly pleased that she had somehow recovered from her ordeal.

As they crossed the last few miles of desert separating them from the border, the late afternoon sun still hot on their backs, he marveled at the power of prayer and wondered whether, if he had not chosen such a violent path, he would still have lost faith.

22

After crossing the border into New Mexico they camped for the night in a remote dry gulch; then, rising early, they rode another half-day until they reached the outskirts of Santa Rosa.

Directly ahead of them stretched the Rio Grande. The river, slowly winding its way south from Las Cruces to El Paso before crossing into Mexico and becoming the Rio Bravo, was less than fifty yards wide here and shallow enough to ford on horseback.

Gabriel and Ellen dismounted beside a thicket of yuccas and let their horses drink while they talked in the shade.

'I'll wait here for 'em,' he told her. 'You ride on into town. Once you spread the word why you're there, it shouldn't take more than a few hours for it to reach the Double SS. Then it's just a matter of me bracing 'em 'fore they cross the river.'

'But what if they don't come this way?'

'They will. It's the shortest way into town and knowin' Slade like I do, once he hears you're waitin' for a gunfighter to arrive on the mornin' train, he'll want to get to you as soon as possible.'

'And if they're already in town — then what?'

She sounded uneasy, and he wondered why.

'We've already discussed that.'

'I know, I know, but tell me again. I'm so nervous, Gabe, I can barely remember my own name.'

'You hole up in the Carlisle Hotel and wait for me. Don't open your door to anyone. If Slade and the Iversons don't ride in by sundown, I'll know they're already in town. Then I'll come in fast, and force a showdown with them.'

'No, no,' she exclaimed, 'you can't come into Santa Rosa.'

'I don't have a choice.'

'But someone will recognize you and tell Sheriff Forbes. Then he'll arrest you.'

'He'll try.'

'More killing? Good God, is that what you want?'

'What I want,' he reminded grimly, 'is what you want: Slade and the Iversons dead.'

But did she? Her growing uneasiness worried him.

'OK,' he said, trying to be patient, 'tell you what: if I do have to come in, I'll wait till after dark. That way, chances are nobody will see me until the gunplay's over.'

'And then what? You think you can just ride out before the sheriff and his deputies show up? After shooting three men in front of the whole town? Why, you wouldn't have a prayer. You'd be shot to ribbons before you reached your horse.'

'Simmer down,' he said, seeing how upset she was. 'We've gone over this a hundred times, Ellie. Trust me. It's the best way to handle it.'

She was silent a long time. He could tell something was eating at her and he wondered what it was.

'No,' she said suddenly, 'the best way is to call everything off. For us to ride north, straight on up to Las Cruces and stay with Grampa Tate. His spread is way out of town. No one will ever know you're around.'

He couldn't believe his ears. ' 'Mean, forget all about Slade an' the Iversons altogether?'

'Yes, yes,' Ellen said. 'Grampa Tate would love me to stay with him. And I know he'd like to meet you, too.'

'Kind of late to be changin' horses.'

'I know. But Cally would understand, Gabe, I know she would. In fact she'd want me to forget it. She hated killing as much as I do, and . . . now that I actually think of it, of actually having you kill someone on my account or even Cally's, I don't think I can go through with it. In fact I know I can't. It's too horrible to even contemplate.

Do you understand what I'm saying, Gabe?'

'No,' he said after a long pause. 'I don't understand any of it. But then I ain't a woman. An' it wasn't my sister who was raped and murdered. So how could I?'

'Being a woman hasn't anything to do with it.'

'It has everythin' to do with it. I'm not slighting women — most I've known were tougher than men in many ways or they couldn't have stood givin' birth. But they didn't know diddly squat about killing. Their men handled it for 'em. That's not to say men enjoy killing. Most don't. But we do understand it. It's taught to us when we're young'uns an' it sticks with us all the way through till we're toes up in the dirt. If you were a man you'd understand that.'

She didn't say anything.

'Escalero understood — that's why he gave his life for you.'

'Don't you think I know that?' she

said angrily. 'Don't you think I won't be carrying the guilt of his death — his and Cerrildo's — for the rest of my days?'

Right now, he wasn't sure what to think. An Apache on mescal could not have been more confusing.

'But two wrongs don't make a right,' she continued. 'Miguel would have understood that, too. He was closer to God than I ever was. In fact, during the ride he begged me to turn around and go back to the convent, more times than you can count. Killing Slade and the Iversons was wrong, he kept saying. No matter what they did or how despicable they were, or how much I wanted them dead, I shouldn't — '

'Sweet Judas!' Gabriel said, suddenly realizing. 'It was at the church, wasn't it?'

'Church?'

'Back there at Cohiba, when you were praying? What happened, Ellie? Did you confess to the padre and he made you see the light of God?'

She avoided his gaze and he knew he'd hit pay dirt.

'Killing is wrong,' she said quietly. 'I've known that all along. But all I could think of was revenge ... of getting even for Cally's sake. But when I talked to Padre Felipe — '

'He put you in touch with your conscience?'

She let all her feelings out in a long troubled sigh.

'Perhaps. I honestly don't know. I do know killing is wrong and at the same time I know, God help me, I still want Slade and the Iversons dead. I just don't know if I can be the one to kill them. Or worse, have you kill them for me. Oh Gabe,' she said miserably, 'I know how crazy I must sound. I can't even believe what I'm saying myself. For weeks now I've been so consumed with hatred and the idea of avenging Cally, I couldn't think of anything else. But now — now, I'm not so sure. I'm so confused I don't know what to do. I can't even think straight any more.'

He gazed up into her face, into her distraught, pain-filled violet eyes and saw she was telling the truth. Immediately he knew what he had to do.

'Then I'll have to think for you, Ellie. For both of us, I reckon.'

'Yes,' she said wearily. 'You will. You must.'

He swung up into the saddle and waited for her to remount before spurring the Morgan down the muddy bank and on into the river in the direction of Santa Rosa.

23

As they crossed the railroad tracks and entered the hot dusty town from the south, the wind changed direction — now it was in their faces and they could smell the stock-yards. They rode past the holding-pens, the lowing of the densely packed cattle sounding like a desert wind, and turned onto Main Street.

'Things haven't changed much,' Gabriel said. 'Cattle still stink an' most of 'em still wear a Double SS brand.'

'And Santa Rosa still owes its existence to Stadtlander's money,' Ellen reminded him. 'Including — no, especially — the law.'

Gabriel grunted. 'If you're tryin' to scare me into changing my mind, Ellie, it ain't workin'.'

As they made their way between the oncoming buck-boards and other riders, Gabriel realized little had changed during his five-year absence. Main Street was still unpaved and rutted by heavy freight wagons; and though the boardwalks had recently been widened, allowing people to pass one another without bumping shoulders, the hotels, cantinas, stores, livery stables, law offices and barber-shops lining them still looked familiar.

Unfortunately, he hadn't changed much either. And he and Ellen had barely entered town when a passerby recognized him.

After a quick double take, the elderly woman ducked into Melvin's Haber-dashery and within moments she, the owner and several customers reap-peared, eyes saucers, mouths agape, and watched as Gabriel and Ellen rode on up the street.

Faster than a common cold, word spread through town that Mesquite Jennings was back.

Shoppers turned to watch him and Ellen ride past.

Riders twisted in their saddles to get a second look.

Alarmed mothers dragged their struggling children away.

Street urchins ran alongside Gabriel, hands held like pistols, shooting each other and dying in gasping, dramatic ways.

'Bang! Bang! Bang!'

'Yer dead, Mesquite,' one kid screamed at another.

'No, I ain't, Sheriff. I shot you first!'

'Didn't.'

'Did, too!'

Gabriel ignored them. But Ellen, distressed by their yelling, shouted at them to go away.

Her anger only fed their curiosity.

'You a outlaw too?' a carrot-haired, gap-toothed boy asked her. 'Are ya, are ya, are ya?' he demanded when she looked away. 'I bet you are.'

'How many people you shot?' asked another.

'She ain't shot any,' his friend said. 'How could she? She ain't even wearin' a gun!'

'But he is,' said the redhead, pointing

195

at Gabriel. 'An' I bet he's shot more'n a hundred.'

Upset, Ellen kicked the roan into a faster gait.

'Little monsters,' she said when Gabriel caught up to her. 'They act like you're some kind of carnival freak. Please,' she begged when he didn't answer, 'let's ride out of here while you still have the chance.'

'I'm done runnin',' was all he said. They rode on.

★ ★ ★

A few minutes later a deputy spotted them tying their horses to the rail fronting the Carlisle Hotel.

He froze in his tracks, praying that Gabriel hadn't seen him and at the same time making sure his hands weren't near his six-gun. He wasn't pulling down enough wages to challenge a professional gunfighter; especially one who had reputedly killed ten men.

Waiting until they entered the hotel,

he sprinted to the office to notify Sheriff Forbes that his old nemesis was back.

⋆ ⋆ ⋆

The desk clerk at the Carlisle Hotel was equally intimidated.

A prissy young Nellie with yellow hair slicked down with lilac-scented tonic, he was so sugary polite and ingratiating that Gabriel eventually lost his temper. Grabbing him by the lapels, he pulled his face close and said:

'Quit runnin' your mouth, you little squirt, an' hand over the damn room key!'

Terrified, the clerk obeyed.

'W-Will there be anything else, sir?' he stammered.

'Yeah, I need you to get a case of the forgets.'

'Sir?'

'If anybody asks you which room Miss Kincaide's in, you tell 'em you don't remember. Savvy?'

'But, sir — '

' 'Specially anybody who rides for the Double SS. You got that? You don't remember!'

'Yes, sir. I understand, sir. Perfectly, sir. Thank you, sir. Thank you very much. Enjoy your stay.' He watched his guests climb the stairs to the second floor and then had to sit down before he fainted.

★　★　★

Room 214 was small, clean and comfortable with a window overlooking Main Street. Gabriel pulled the sun-faded curtain back enough so he could watch what was going on outside, and saw a gangling young rider gallop out of town. His deputy star glinted in the sunlight and Gabriel guessed he was headed out to the Double SS. He knew then that any chance of surprising Stadtlander was gone. Now, when he rode out to the ranch, they would be waiting for him.

As if reading his mind, Ellen clutched his arm and begged him to change his mind.

He ignored her and continued staring out the window.

'Please, Gabe, you don't have to do this. There's still time for us to ride out of here or to catch the 4:17 to Las Cruces. Please,' she said when he didn't answer. 'I'm begging you. Oh dear God, why won't you listen to reason?'

He turned from the window, cupped his rough hands about her face, and studied her with his flinty blue eyes.

'If I agree,' he said softly, 'will you come with me?'

'Of course.'

'I don't just mean to Las Cruces.'

His remark caught her by surprise.

'W-Where then?'

'Arizona. Texas. Maybe even California. Don't matter much where or which direction. Just so we keep one jump ahead of the posse.'

She hesitated, suddenly realizing he was asking her to run away with him. It wasn't the life she wanted, but unable to face the thought of being responsible for the death of a third man, she said bravely:

'Yes. Of course I will.'

'I got your word on that?'

'Yes.'

'An' the convent . . . your vows to the church an' desire to do God's work . . . you'll sweep all that under the rug?'

She nodded, unable to actually say the words.

He searched her face with his eyes for another moment and then gently kissed her on the lips.

She tried to respond, but much as she cared for him it was useless. She had already given herself to another.

Gabriel smiled gratefully at her.

'I figured as much.'

'Wait,' she said as he walked to the door. 'Where're you going?'

'Where you can't.'

'To brace Stadtlander?'

He nodded, tight-lipped.

'I don't understand. What about us? I

thought you just said . . . asked me to run off with you?'

'An' you lied 'bout as well as anyone could.'

'I wasn't — '

'An' for that I thank you.'

She realized he'd only been testing her.

'That wasn't fair, Gabe.'

Sorry for embarrassing her, he said: 'I had to know.'

'What if I'd been serious?'

'I still would've told you no.' His voice gentled. 'You're a fine woman, Ellie. I could do no better. But like I told your sister: it wouldn't work. Bein' on the run's akin to no life at all. It wears on you, drags you down no matter who you are.'

Surprised, Ellen said: 'Cally wanted to go? She never told me that.'

'No reason to. How we felt about each other, that was between us.' He put his hat on and opened the door. 'Now, you go wash up an' then get on the train, Ellie. Get on that train an' go back to the convent. Do what you were born for. An' I'll do the same.'

'Gabe . . . '

He stopped, halfway out the door.

' . . . I'm sorry.'

'For what? Tryin' to save my life?' He smiled. ''Cept for Cally, you're the only person ever cared enough to do that.' He was gone before she could say anything.

Ellen moved to the door, looked out and along the green-walled hallway and saw him descending the stairs. She hoped he would look back, maybe even wave good-bye, but he did neither.

Eyes stinging with tears, she sadly closed the door.

24

Emerging from the hotel, Gabriel paused on the board-walk and looked around. He half-expected to find Sheriff Forbes with his deputies gathered in the street, waiting for him with their scatter-guns ready.

But there wasn't a lawman in sight. No-good gutless bastard, Gabriel thought. He's goin' to stay out of sight an' let Stadtlander do his dirty work for him.

He turned into the sun, pulled his hat low over his eyes and walked back to the livery stable. Oncoming pedestrians quickly stepped out of his way and then looked back for a moment, awed by the sight of the infamous gunfighter. With Billy the Kid in his grave, John Wesley Hardin doing time in a Texas prison, and Holliday and the Earp brothers merely a memory at Tombstone, Mesquite Jennings was the last of a vanishing breed.

Gabriel paid no attention to them. But it was two blocks to the livery stable and he couldn't help hearing their whispers.

'That's him!'

'You sure?'

''Course I'm sure. That's Mesquite Jennings, all right.'

'Can you believe it? Walkin' down Main Street bold as brass.'

'Didn't he use to ride for the Double SS?'

'Sure. Four, maybe five years ago.'

'Still be workin' there most likely, if'n he hadn't stole Mr Stadtlander's favorite horse.'

'I heard there was a noose waitin' for him every place he went after that.'

'Still is.'

'Then what the hell's he doin' back here?'

'Yeah, an' who's the woman with him?'

'Probably some whore he picked up. Like the Kid, he always did have a soft spot for cheap whiskey an' round-heeled women.'

Controlling an urge to pistol-whip the last speaker, Gabriel crossed the street to Lars Gustafson's livery. There, pausing outside the big open door, he glanced back to make sure he hadn't been followed. When he was satisfied he was safe, he entered the stable and paid the club-footed hostler for feeding and watering the horses.

'What about the roan, Mr Jennings, sir? What you want me to do with her?'

'Keep her here till Miss Kincaide comes by.' Gabriel handed the hostler extra money. 'She may want you to hang onto her for a spell, or sell her. I don't know. But anythin' the lady asks you to do, do it, OK? Free of charge an' with a big friendly smile.'

'Yessir, Mr Jennings. You can count on me, sir. Anythin' else, sir?'

'Those two smokes you got in your pocket — how much?'

'For you, Mr Jennings — nothin'. No charge at all. Hell, it's an honor just to know you smoked 'em.'

He watched the tall, rangy gunfighter

step into the saddle and ride off.

Mesquite Jennings, he said to himself. I'll be damned. He whistled softly knowing that one day, when his kids grew up and had young'uns of their own, he'd gather them all around him and tell them the story of the day that he, Thomas Edwin Madden, gave New Mexico's most famous outlaw since Billy the Kid his last two cigars.

25

As he rode away from the stable, turned onto Lower Front Street and continued through the poorer section of Santa Rosa, Gabriel looked up and saw three of Mama Rosita's whores watching him intently from an open window above the Copper Palace.

He didn't recognize any of them, but he grinned and tipped his hat anyway and was surprised when they didn't respond. Whores made most of their money from repeat business and ignoring strangers wasn't smart or customary.

Blaming it on his reputation, he took out one of the hostler's cheap cigars, bit the end off and stuck it in his mouth. As he went to fire a match on the saddle horn he saw a glint of metal in the alley next to the Copper Palace.

Instinctively, he threw himself sideways, freeing his boots from the stirrups and leaping out of the saddle on the other side of the horse — hearing as he did the familiar 'pa-a-anng!' of a rifle.

A second later he hit the ground. Keeping his momentum going by rolling over, he came up on one knee and, gun already in hand, fired twice under the belly of the Morgan at a figure crouched in the mouth of the alley.

The man dropped his Winchester, stumbled back and collapsed in the dirt.

Gabriel scrambled across the street and dived behind a public water trough.

More gunfire came from across the street. Bullets and shotgun slugs thunked into the trough near his head. As he peered around the side he saw Slade Stadtlander and the younger of the Iverson brothers, Cody, firing at him from the entrance of the Copper Palace.

Gabriel knew Slade was a better shot, but he was shooting a six-gun, while Cody was blasting at him with a scattergun. The choice was simple.

Gabriel waited until he'd fired both barrels, the heavy slugs tearing chunks of wood from the trough, and then stood up and fanned three shots at the bearded Iverson.

Cody took them in the chest. He staggered back as if pushed by a giant hand, dropped his 12-gauge and crumpled onto his face.

Shocked by Cody's death, Slade hastily emptied his .45 at Gabriel, turned and ran back into the saloon.

Gabriel crossed the street, reloading as he walked. He was pissed at himself. Before he'd holed up in Mexico he would never have been caught off-guard like that; he would have expected word of his presence to have spread to every saloon and whorehouse in Santa Rosa — and, as a result, would have anticipated someone to come gunning for him. Either some punk kid gunslinger, anxious to make a fast reputation for himself, or maybe a bounty hunter; or even one of Sheriff Forbes's deputies, who were known to be backshooters.

Instead, he'd grown complacent and had narrowly escaped being shot down in broad daylight. Well, he promised himself grimly, it sure as hell wouldn't happen again.

He mounted the boardwalk and paused at the entrance to the venerable old saloon and gambling palace. Then he stepped to one side and peered over the batwing doors.

Inside, everyone was trying to look normal as they either stood drinking at the long half-moon bar or played poker or faro in the casino in back.

A little too normal, Gabriel thought. He glanced up at the balcony leading to the whores' rooms, and saw a couple of cowboys talking to a straw-haired woman who looked fat and sweaty in red satin.

Deciding not to risk falling into a trap, Gabriel walked to the alley and knelt beside the man he'd shot earlier. As he rolled him over with his boot, he saw it was the older Iverson, Mace.

His eyelids fluttered and Gabriel

realized he was still alive. Kneeling, he put his lips against Mace's ear and whispered:

'This is for Cally . . . ' and shot him in the forehead.

The booming echo of the shot was still reverberating in the alley when Gabriel heard the sound of a horse galloping away. He ran to the end of the alley and peered over the fence — in time to see Slade riding off in the direction of the Double SS.

So, Gabriel thought as he ejected the spent shells and reloaded the Peace-maker. It's all going to end at the same place it started.

26

With the hubbub of Santa Rosa fading behind him, Gabriel picked up the trail leading out to the Double SS and kicked the stallion into a mile-consuming lope. The Morgan was more co-operative than he'd expected it to be after the spurring he'd given it in San Dimas, and leery of its penchant for payback he kept a watchful eye on its behavior as they rode across the hot open wasteland.

In a way it was a blessing, he thought. Having to worry about being bucked off gave him something to think of besides the trouble he knew was waiting for him at Stadtlander's.

* * *

It was an hour's ride to the high, arched, signature gateway that warned everyone they were entering Double SS land; and then another twenty minute climb up to the crest of the flat-topped knoll on which stood the rancher's impressive, Western-style mansion.

Stadtlander had chosen to build his home atop the grassy knoll for two reasons: at first, in the early days, so he could see his enemies coming; and later, when with Gabriel's help he'd forced out all the other ranchers and could afford to replace the original modest, single-story ranch house with a fancy three-story mansion, to let the rest of the world see how rich and important he'd become.

Now, as Gabriel nudged the Morgan up the long grassy incline, he knew a dozen or more unfriendly pairs of eyes were watching him. But he felt perfectly safe. Stadtlander was many things, most of them bad, but he was no back-shooter or bushwhacker. Unlike his sly, mealy-mouthed son, Slade, if the Old Man was going to kill you he wanted to look you in the eyes as he pulled the trigger.

As Gabriel rode slowly uphill, his gaze fixed ahead on the familiar ranch house and various outer buildings surrounding it, he felt a sense of coming home. Mixed emotions came with the feeling. Despite his deep-rooted anger at Stadtlander for wrongfully branding him a horse-thief and destroying any chance he had of a normal future, Gabriel felt a strange, warm attachment for the irascible, gruff rancher.

He knew he owed him a lot.

Since that bleak wintry morning almost ten years ago, with the ground frosted rock-hard and covered in patches with snow, when as a raw, quick-tempered youth 'Gabe' had hired on as a hand at the Double SS, he had felt he belonged there.

It didn't take long before other people felt the same way. The fact that he could sign his name rather than just make a mark, like most of the semi-illiterate hands, set him apart. It also brought him to Stadtlander's attention.

'I hear you can read'n write, boy?' the

short, powerfully built rancher said to him a few days after he'd been hired.

'Yes, sir.'

'I also hear you got a mighty quick temper — that true?'

Gabriel shrugged.

'Speak up, boy. When I ask you a question I expect an answer.'

'I stand up for m'self, sir, that's all.'

Stadtlander studied him, a hand-rolled smoke protruding from under his brown, droopy, gunfighter's mustache.

'I got no quarrel with that,' he said gruffly. 'But I checked around, an' accordin' to Sheriff Forbes and his deputies it goes a mite further than that. Seems, they think you're carryin' a chip and just itchin' for someone to try an' knock it off.'

Gabriel shrugged again.

'I'm not responsible for how folks think, Mr Stadtlander. I mind my own business an' I expect others to do the same.'

'An' when they don't, you're happy to teach 'em some manners, that it?

Don't answer that,' Stadtlander added wryly. 'I don't possess the sweetest disposition myself so I know all about learnin' people manners. But what I do want to know, boy, is if that iron on your hip is for show or to back up what your fists can't handle.'

'So far,' Gabriel replied, 'I ain't found nobody these fists can't handle.'

Stadtlander chuckled. 'Modest son-of-a-buck, aren't you?' As he spoke he suddenly went for his gun. His draw wouldn't have scared Hickok or Clay Allison but it was still plenty fast — which is why he was surprised to find himself staring at the old Walker Colt held by the youngster in front of him.

'That modest enough for you, Mr Stadlander?'

For a second Stadtlander didn't respond; then he laughed, loud and hearty, and lifted his hand from his still-holstered six-gun.

'I like a man who can best me,' he said. 'Just so he's workin' for me an' not agin me.' He waited for Gabriel to holster his gun and then drove his fist, with all his might, into the youth's jaw.

Gabriel went sprawling and lay there, flat on his back on the cowhide rug, stunned.

'Next time you point a pistol at me, son,' Stadtlander said without rancor, 'be ready to shoot it.'

'I'll remember that,' Gabriel promised, groggily getting to his feet. 'Don't think I won't.'

Now, as Gabriel rode past the outer corrals and on between the barn and two bunkhouses, he thought about his promise and gripped the butt of his Peacemaker as if to remind himself not to be caught off-guard again.

Meanwhile the Morgan, as if aware that it had returned to familiar surroundings, pricked it ears and snorted uneasily.

'Easy,' Gabriel told it softly. 'Don't sunfish on me now, horse.'

Ahead, a war party of some twenty armed ranch hands waited for him in front of the mansion. Behind them, standing on the top step of a wide veranda that ran all the way around the big square house, was Stadtlander's son, Slade.

'He's here, Pa,' Gabriel heard him call out.

Gabriel rode closer, now trapped in the giant shadow cast by the mansion.

The front door opened and out limped Stillman J. Stadtlander.

Thinner than Gabriel remembered, the seventy-one-year-old rancher's thick, wavy brown hair had turned all white and his square, jut-jawed face was now deeply lined, especially around the eyes and down-turned mouth. He'd also become stoop-shouldered and was plagued by gout, needing a cane to help him walk.

But as he stood beside his son on the top step, Gabriel barely noticed any of those things: it was the old man's eyes that grabbed his attention. Once burning with fire and defiance, they now looked dim and sad as if years of sorrow and disillusionment had finally worn him down.

But despite his appearance, Gabriel knew he was still tougher than most men.

The cowhands parted as Gabriel drew near, allowing him to ride up to the front steps. They then closed ranks again, forming a half-circle behind him, rifles held ready.

Gabriel reined up the Morgan and remained in the saddle as he confronted father and son.

'See you finally brought my horse back,' Stadtlander said making no attempt to greet him.

Gabriel smiled mirthlessly. 'Just wanted him to see what he was missin'.'

Stung by his sarcasm, Stadtlander thrust his jaw out belligerently. 'An' you, boy, look about you, see what you gave up too.'

'Not gave up, was took from.'

'Aces'n eights,' Stadtlander said with a hint of regret. 'Two pair beats a pair every time. How well I remember.'

Slade cut in angrily. 'Don't waste your breath on him, Pa. Just say the word an' I'll get a rope. Show him what we do to backshooters.'

Stadtlander impatiently motioned for him to be quiet and then turned back to Gabriel.

'You know me, Gabe. I've never hung anybody without first lettin' him have his say. So speak your piece. Tell me true how it played out between you'n the Iversons.'

'You haven't seen their bodies?'

'Ain't been off the ranch in nigh on a week.'

'Then I reckon you don't know your son's a damn' liar.'

There was silence. The cowhands looked expectantly at Slade.

Seething, he inched his hand toward his six-gun. But, as always, fear of Gabriel stopped him from drawing.

'You ain't baitin' me into a fight,' he told Gabriel. 'I'm gonna have too much fun watchin' you swing.'

Embarrassed for him, the cowhands looked at their feet.

Stadtlander scowled contemptuously

at Slade and then told Gabriel: 'I'm still waitin' to hear your side.'

Keeping an eye on Slade, Gabriel described how Cory, Mace and Slade had ambushed him outside the Copper Palace.

Several times Slade tried to interrupt, but always his father waved him silent.

When Gabriel was finished, Stadtlander eyed his son suspiciously.

'You told me he came up behind Cory an' Mace in the alley beside the Copper Palace.'

'He did, Pa. I swear. Sneaked up an' shot 'em 'fore they even knew he was there. Ask anyone. They'll say how it happened.'

'If that's true,' Gabriel said quietly, 'then maybe you can explain how the entry wounds are in their chests, not their backs.'

The last three words were addressed to Stadtlander, who looked disgustedly at his son.

'You tellin' me fish stories, boy?'

'No, Pa. I ain't. Honest. Am I, boys?'

he said to the men gathered before him. 'Some of you were in town this mornin'. Tell him how it happened.'

The men hesitated and shifted uncomfortably on their feet. Stadtlander glared at them. Under his steely-eyed gaze they all wilted and quickly looked away.

Enraged, Stadtlander grabbed Slade by the shirt front and shook him.

'Damn you, you snivelin' pup! Ain't you ever gonna quit lyin' to me?'

'Pa, don't ride me like that in front of — '

Stadtlander backhanded him across the mouth.

'Bite your tongue, boy! 'Fore I take a whip to you!' He pushed his son roughly away. 'You're mighty tough when it comes to bullyin' whores an' folks who can't fight back — '

'Pa, I'm warnin' you — '

'Come up against a real man an' most likely you'd piss your pants.'

Pushed to a fury, Slade reached for his six-gun.

But Stadtlander was too fast for him. Knocking the gun from Slade's hand, he slapped him, kept slapping him, hard vicious blows that spun his head from side to side until the men couldn't watch any more.

'That's enough,' Gabriel said at last.

Stadtlander went to slap his dazed son again, then stopped and looked around as if suddenly realizing where he was and what he was doing. As his rage subsided he shoved his son aside, saying:

'All mouth, that's what you are, boy. Kind of snake who spends his life whistlin' 'round gravestones.'

'Pa — '

'Gutless to the bone. Always have been. Why, even your ma, God rest her soul, knew that. That's why she protected you — why I'm protectin' you now.'

'From what?' Slade whined. 'I didn't do nothin' to need no protectin'.'

'Except rape an' kill a decent woman,' Gabriel said grimly. He kept his eyes on both father and son as he spoke, ready to shoot whichever man drew first.

Stadtlander turned to him. 'So *that's* why you're here? I been tryin' to figure out your reason ever since I heard you was back.'

'Well, now you know,' Gabriel said. 'So you can quit actin' surprised.'

'What I know,' Stadtlander said, 'is you've made a long ride for nothin'. My boy's innocent.'

'Quit wastin' time, Pa,' Slade said picking up his gun. 'Let me get a — '

'Button it,' Stadtlander told him angrily. Then to Gabriel: 'All you got to do is read Sheriff Forbes's written statement: says clear as day there wasn't any reason to accuse Slade or the Iversons of rape or murder since they were right here, at the ranch, playin' — '

'Five-card stud, yeah I heard,' Gabriel said. 'But we both know that's a day's ride from the truth.'

'Pa, ain't you heard enough?' Slade said. 'Let me go get a rope.'

Stadtlander looked at him with withering disgust.

'Are you loco as well as a liar?'

'Pa, cut it out! Quit proddin' me.'

'Or what — you'll kill me? That'll be the day.' Stadtlander turned to Gabriel. 'See what I've raised? Boy's got squirrel fur for brains. Don't even know when death's starin' him in the face.'

He glared at his son as if hoping he had the guts to shoot him. But Slade never moved.

'Hell's fire, boy,' Stadtlander barked at him, 'don't you get it? I'm all you got. I move aside or let you take one step toward a rope an' the next voice you'll hear will be a minister readin' over your grave. You want that, boy? Huh? You want him to shoot you? 'Cause if you do, just say the word an' I'll order the men back to work an' let you two make your play. I didn't think so,' he said when Slade looked away. 'Well, maybe I was wrong about you. Maybe you do have some brains after all.' Turning back to Gabriel he added:

'Come inside. I'll build you a drink.'

'I'd sooner not — '

'I ain't askin' you, dammit, I'm tellin' you. Let's talk this over like men. You owe me that, Gabe, at least.' Without waiting for a reply, he stormed indoors.

Gabriel, his eyes never leaving Slade, slowly stepped from the saddle and followed him.

27

Stadtlander's study took up a whole corner of the mansion. The huge oak-paneled room had windows on two sides, one facing the scrubland on which his vast herd grazed and the other with a panoramic view of the distant Rio Grande. Western paintings and deer and elk trophy heads adorned the walls, and grizzly pelts covered the stained-wood floor.

The massive furniture was covered in brown-and-white cowhide and there was enough room in the stone fireplace to spit-roast a whole steer. Above it hung an imposing painting of Stadtlander astride the Morgan in an 'empire builder' pose, while facing him across the room hung an equally impressive painting of his deceased wife, Agatha. A pale, delicate, sweet-faced Easterner of obvious fine breeding, she seemed out of place in this testosterone-filled atmosphere.

Hanging beside her, one on either side, were smaller portraits of Slade and his deceased sister, Elizabeth, both in their early teens.

Stadtlander limped behind the bar that stretched along one wall and poured them both tumblers of J.H. Cutler.

'To better times,' he said.

Gabriel ignored the toast, drank and looked around at all the familiar memorabilia. Much as he hated to admit it, he loved this room and had always hoped that one day he would build one of his own just like it.

Stadtlander pushed a humidor of expensive Cuban cigars in front of Gabriel, who shook his head. Ignoring the rebuff, Stadtlander took one himself, snipped off the end with a fancy clipper, wetted it between his lips and took his time lighting it.

'I've missed you, Gabe. I won't deny that.'

He waited for Gabriel to respond in kind. When he didn't, Stadtlander spat out a thin stream of smoke and contemplated the ash forming on his cigar.

'That boy I raised — he's a daisy, ain't he?'

Gabriel sipped his whiskey in silence.

'Big, good-lookin' kid . . . can get any woman he wants just like that.' He snapped his fingers. 'Hell, any stranger lookin' at him would think he had the world in his fist . . . '

Gabriel still said nothing.

'Thing that riles me most is, he'll take over this spread one day an' then what? Instead of buildin' it up, makin' it grow like I did, he'll run it into the ground in two, maybe three years. Maybe less.'

He again waited for Gabriel to respond and again Gabriel sipped his whiskey in cold silence.

Stadtlander looked deflated. Using the sleeve of his leather jacket to wipe a wet spot from the polished bar, he gulped his drink and poured himself another.

'I've tried to raise him right,' he said, as if trying to convince himself. 'Taught him to know the difference 'tween right and wrong, but so help me Jonah, he's no closer to bein' a man now than he was when you took off five years ago.'

'Won't matter where he's goin',' Gabriel said grimly.

Stadtlander started to erupt, but thought better of it and said: 'Got a question for you. An' I want a straight answer.'

Gabriel sipped his whiskey and waited.

'What went wrong between us, Gabe? I've asked myself a thousand times but I never could figure it out.'

'I got tired of doin' your dirty work.'

'After almost ten years? Moses on the mountain! By then you'd run everybody off. What was left was more maintenance than work.'

'There were other things.'

'Name one.'

'You demanded too much.'

'No more than I demanded of myself.'

'Yeah, but it was your spread.'

'Could've been yours, too. Mine, yours and Slade's. There was more than enough land to go around. Cattle, too. I told you that many times.'

Gabriel couldn't deny that and kept silent.

'Hell, I thought we were a matched pair. I even groomed you so you could take over when I got too old to run the place. Figured my boy could watch how you did things, see the way you treated people, earned their respect and got the most out of a crew — hopin' that way he'd learn from you before finally takin' over himself.'

Gabriel swirled his whiskey around in the tumbler, held the glass up in front of the window and watched the amber-colored liquid change colors in the sunlight.

'God *dammit,*' Stadtlander said angrily, 'we ain't gonna get anywhere, Gabe, unless you speak your mind; tell me what you think.'

'I think,' Gabriel said evenly, 'you're doin' exactly what you accused Slade of doin': whistling 'round gravestones.'

'How so?'

Gabriel studied Stadtlander, remembering as he did how once he would have jumped into the fires of hell to please him.

''Cause all this talk about yesteryear is just another way of stalling, of duckin' the truth.'

'That's a damn' lie an' you know it! I never ducked the truth or told a lie in my whole life.'

'That include callin' me a horse thief?'

'OK, once. An' I was wrong to do that. I admit it now. You won Brandy fair'n square. But goddammit, Gabe, you gotta take some responsibility for this split. You shouldn't have come at me like that. You know my temper. How'd you expect me to react when the man I've treated better'n my own son threatens to walk out on me — is willin' to throw away everything I've given him on account of some doe-eyed widow in a cantina — '

'Keep Cally out of this,' Gabriel warned, his hand drifting to his gun.

Stadtlander bristled for a moment. Then he saw the deadly, unwavering look in Gabriel's ice blue eyes and subsided.

'As for all the things you say you gave me,' Gabriel continued, 'that's another lie. You gave me nothin'. I earned everythin' I got around here.'

'I ain't denyin' that. That's why I made you top hand.'

'You made me top hand, Mr Stadtlander, 'cause I could handle a gun. If I hadn't been fast, I'd still be mendin' fences an' you know it.'

'Damn you! Why do you always have to spit in my face?'

'You said you wanted the truth. I'm givin' it to you.'

'The truth,' Stadtlander said, 'is you were the son I always wanted an' I was willin' to spurn my own boy, my own flesh and blood to show you how I felt.'

'Sendin' a necktie party after me is a funny way of sayin' you loved me.'

Stadtlander flushed and his temple veins bulged.

'Anger made me do that. Anger an' hurt. When I couldn't change your mind I wanted to destroy you.'

'An' you damn' near succeeded.'

Stadtlander continued as if Gabriel hadn't spoken.

'But all that's over an' done with now. Buried in the past. We're both still alive an' I'm willin' to forget the ill between us if you are. How 'bout it, Gabe?' he said, sticking out his hand. 'You willin' to turn the page? Let bygones be bygones an' start afresh? The Double SS is even bigger now than when you left. One third of it would make you a rich an' powerful man.'

Gabriel ignored the outstretched hand.

'I don't want to be rich an' powerful, Mr Stadtlander.'

'Then what *do* you want?'

'From you — personally — nothin'.'

Rage darkened the old rancher's weathered face.

'Then get the hell off my property. Fast. 'Fore I do like Slade wants and feed you to a rope.'

Gabriel slowly ground out his cigar on the polished bar.

'Only rope you should be worryin' about, Mr Stadtlander, is the one I'm gonna use to hang your son.'

Stadtlander looked at Gabriel in utter disbelief. Then he laughed contemptuously.

'Now that's a hot one,' he said. Leaning over the bar he thrust his face close to Gabriel's. 'Do you really think you can ride out of here with my boy? Why, you arrogant, ungrateful pup, there's more than twenty guns out there all primed to cut you down on my say-so.'

'Then you'd better say-so,' Gabriel said, ''cause I'm leaving now an' I'm takin' Slade with me.'

'Not so long as I'm alive!'

Gabriel walked to the door, turned and looked back at Stadtlander who hadn't moved.

'You once told me that the next time I pointed a gun at you I should be ready to use it. I'm ready.'

Stadtlander started to reply then stopped as he saw Gabriel's Peacemaker — holstered an instant ago — was now aimed at his belly.

He swallowed, hard. 'Go ahead, shoot. You'll be dead 'fore the echo leaves this room.'

'I won't die alone,' was all Gabriel said. Holstering his Colt almost as fast as he'd drawn it, he opened the door and stepped outside.

28

Slade and the cowhands stopped talking and ground out their smokes as Gabriel appeared, followed by Stadtlander.

'Do I get a rope, Pa?' Slade asked him.

'No time for that, son.' Stadtlander raised his voice so his men could hear. 'Mr Moonlight's just been kind enough to tell me why he's here. He's come for you, Slade. Plans on takin' you somewhere nice'n quiet where he can introduce you to a rope.'

Slade licked his lips uneasily and forced himself to laugh.

'' 'Be a sonofabitch,' he said. He winked at the men. 'Hear that, boys? I'm about to dance my last fandango.'

The men laughed.

'Oh, save me, boss, please.' A cowhand grabbed his own bandanna and pulled it above his head, gurgling as he pretended to hang himself.

The other men roared.

Bolstered by their merriment, Slade said: 'We'll see who's gonna do the introducin'.'

He grabbed a rope from a corral fence, uncoiled it, shook out a loop and twirled it deftly. 'Bring him to the barn, boys. Time someone learned him some manners — '

Gabriel drew and fired, so quickly no one realized what had happened until the bullet cut the rope just above the noose.

Everyone froze.

'Tell your men to throw down their guns,' Gabriel said to Stadtlander.

'Go to hell.'

Then as Gabriel cocked the hammer:

'Like I told you inside: go ahead an' shoot. I'm willin' to die to make sure my name's carried on.' He turned to the men. 'Soon as he shoots me, shoot him. Then the horse.'

The cowhands nodded and aimed

their guns at Gabriel.

For one infinitesimal moment time stood still.

Then the Morgan, motionless until now, suddenly reared up and attacked Stadtlander.

One of its flailing hoofs struck the old rancher in the chest, sending him sprawling. He slammed against the veranda railing, then rolled down the steps onto the ground.

Squealing with rage, the stallion reared again intending to trample him.

Without thinking Gabriel quickly grabbed Stadtlander by the boots and dragged him from under the Morgan's descending hoofs.

Brandy turned on him, eyes aflame, teeth bared.

Standing his ground, Gabriel fired twice above the horse's head and yelled at it to get back!

The stallion charged him, ready to bite, but pulled up short before actually making contact with Gabriel. It then stood there in front of him, tossing its head, snorting and pawing angrily at the dirt.

Gabriel, surprised that the Morgan hadn't attacked him, spoke soothingly to it.

It took several seconds, but then the stallion calmed down.

Gabriel helped Stadtlander to his feet. 'Anythin' broke?'

Stadlander winced. 'Rib or two, feels like.'

'Better send someone for the doc.'

'Not before I shoot that ornery bastard!' He turned to the men, adding: 'One of you, toss me your rifle.'

Gabriel thumbed back the hammer on his Colt.

'Anybody harms that horse, deals with me. That includes you,' he said to Stadtlander.

The old rancher saw he meant it.

'It can wait,' he told his men. Wincing at every breath, he started up the steps to the veranda.

Holstering his Colt, Gabriel went to help him.

As he did, Slade shot him in the back.

The bullet glanced off a rib and lodged near Gabriel's spine. He stumbled forward and went to his knees. As he did he pulled his gun and, half-twisting, fired at Slade.

Slade stood there, wide-eyed, as if nothing had happened. Then he pitched forward onto his face, dead before he hit the ground.

Stadtlander looked at his dead son in disbelief; then uttering a low cry, he limped to Slade and cradled him in his arms.

The cowhands angrily surrounded Gabriel, ready to shoot him.

'Say the word, boss,' the foreman said grimly.

Before Stadtlander could answer, there was the sound of a horse approaching.

'Rider comin',' one of the cowhands yelled.

Everyone, including Gabriel, turned and looked.

At first Gabriel thought he was

241

imagining things. But the rider kept on coming, getting closer and closer, passing first between the two outer corrals and then the barn and the bunkhouse, until at last he had to admit to himself the image was real.

It was Ellen.

Astride the blue roan.

She was wearing a black nun's habit, her white hat flopping in the wind.

As she rode up to the astonished cowhands, they grudgingly moved aside to let her pass through.

Ellen rode by without looking at them and reined up beside Gabriel. She dismounted, then saw the blood seeping through the back of his shirt. She moved quickly moved to support him.

'Is it bad?' she asked, worried.

He shook his head and managed to grin.

'Just another scar to lie about.'

'D-Do you think you can you ride?'

'Sure.'

'Then hurry. We must get you to a doctor.'

'He ain't goin' anywhere,' Stadtlander said, still cradling his dead son.

Ellen faced him defiantly.

'What're you talking about? Can't you see he's hurt?'

'I also see my boy's dead. Gabe's gotta pay for that.'

Ellen looked long and hard at him.

'Ever read the Bible, Mr Stadtlander?'

'Live by it.'

'Then I shouldn't have to explain 'an eye for an eye'.'

'Your sister for my son? That's no fair trade.'

'No,' Ellen said, 'it isn't. But it's better than nothing and I'll just have to live with it.' She went to help Gabriel mount up.

The cowhands cocked their weapons, ready to obey Stadtlander's next order.

Gabriel knew his time had run out.

'Step back, Ellie,' he told her. 'Get on your horse and ride out of here.'

Ignoring him, she said to Stadtlander: 'Hasn't there been enough killing

— even for you?'

He glared at her in gritted silence.

'Very well,' she said. 'If you have to spill more blood, tell your men to shoot me, too. Because like it or not, I'm taking Gabe to the doctor.' Turning her back to him, she gently draped Gabriel's arm over her shoulder and helped him limp to the Morgan.

Hesitant to shoot a nun, the men turned to Stadtlander.

'Boss?'

Stadtlander struggled with his conscience. He looked at Gabriel standing bleeding before him, then at Ellen, determined to defy him, and last of all at Slade, dead in his arms.

Suddenly, all the fight went out of him. He seemed to grow smaller. And with a deep sigh, he waved his men back.

'Let him go.'

'But, boss, he killed Slade.'

'And Mace an' Cody, too.'

Stadtlander gently brushed a fly from his dead son's face before answering.

'Can any one of you tell me they didn't deserve it?'

The cowhands looked at one another, stumped.

Stadtlander kept his arms clasped about Slade's corpse and slowly rocked in grief.

'You ever set foot in New Mexico again,' he told Gabriel, now astride the Morgan, 'I swear I'll find a way to kill you.'

'Fair enough.' Gabriel gave a last look at the familiar buildings he'd once called home, and then nudged the Morgan forward.

Ellen did the same to the blue roan.

Stadtlander watched them ride off. Then oblivious of his broken ribs, he got to his knees and tucked one arm under Slade's body.

'Hank . . . Jonas . . . Tom . . . help me carry my boy inside.'

29

The two of them rode side by side down the long steep slope from the top of the knoll.

Every stride the Morgan took felt like a knife-stab in Gabriel's lower back. But not wanting Ellie to know how much pain he was in, he gritted his teeth and looked straight ahead as if nothing were wrong.

But once they had passed under the arched entrance to the Double SS and were out on free range, he knew he couldn't hide it from her much longer. If he was going to say goodbye, he knew he had to do it quickly.

'What's wrong?' she asked as he reined up. 'Can't you ride any further?'

'Sure. But first I'd like to know why — '

' — I'm not on my way to Las Cruces?'

Gabriel nodded and shifted painfully in the saddle.

'Well, I fully intended to catch the train. But as I was leaving the hotel I ran into Sheriff Forbes and two of his deputies. They said you had killed the Iversons.'

'They gave me no choice, Ellie — '

'Oh, I'm not blaming you, Gabe. In fact, hateful as it sounds, I'm glad they're dead. It's just that as I started walking to the tracks, I began thinking . . . worrying about you and . . . Is that who shot you, one of the Iversons?'

'Uh-uh. Slade.' He paused, trying to ignore the burning sensation in his lower back; then, thinking aloud, said: 'Damn fool. I must be gettin' old. Time was I never would've turned my back on a snake like that.'

'Well, you won't have to worry about him or his kind any more,' Ellen said. 'It's over now. For everyone. Now Cally can rest in peace and we can get on with our lives . . . ' She saw him wince and, concerned by how large the bloodstain on his shirt had gotten, said: 'Gabe, we have to hurry. You're losing a lot of blood.'

He ignored her. Numbness was slowly replacing the pain between his spine and the wound — not a good sign.

'Your outfit,' he said. 'Where'd you get it?'

'One of the sisters at Mission Santa Rosa loaned it to me.' She smiled wanly. 'It took some persuading but I thought a little help from God might come in handy.'

He didn't say anything. His eyes went glassy and he felt himself drifting off.

The Morgan, as if sensing something was wrong, snorted and shifted restlessly on its feet.

Jolted back to reality, Gabriel shook the cobwebs from his head and grinned.

'Rescued by a nun,' he said. ' . . . if that ain't one for the cavalry.'

Blood was now seeping through his Levis onto the Morgan's flank.

'Please, Gabe,' Ellen begged, grasping his arm, 'no more talking. We must get you to the doctor — '

'No doctor,' he said firmly.

'W-What're you talking about? If you don't get that wound taken care of you could die.'

'I told you, it ain't that bad. Just a lot of blood is all. Day or two it'll heal on its own.'

'Or you could be dead.'

'Ellie, right now I don't have time for doctors. No,' he said as she started to protest, 'let me finish. You don't know Stillman Stadtlander like I do. In a little while he's gonna regret lettin' me ride out of there. Then he'll get to ragin' an' send his men after me. Maybe even whip up a posse. Only chance I got of dodgin' a rope is to get a good jump on 'em.'

'Then we'll take the train — '

'Next train's tomorrow mornin', Ellie. By then I won't need patchin' up.'

'Then we'll go to the mission. I'm sure Father Quivira will hide you . . . '

she broke off, realizing by his tight-lipped expression that he wasn't going to change his mind.

'Where will you go?'

'California.'

'But that's so far away. We might never see each other again.'

'I thought about that. They have lots of missions out there. All up an' down the coast. My pa was always talkin' about them. Said they were built by this padre from Spain who made believers out of the Indians.'

'Father Serre?'

'Yeah, that's him.' Gabriel felt his tongue grow thick and unmanageable. He coughed, spat away the blood and said: 'Maybe later, after you get to be a proper nun, you could find a way to transfer to one of 'em. Then I could ride over an' visit you all the time.'

She sensed he was lying but said anyway:

'That'd be wonderful. But how will you know which one I'm in?'

'I'll write you at the convent. Let you

know where I am.'

The numbness was spreading up his spine and starting to affect his left arm. He knew time was running out.

'I better ride,' he said.

'Promise you'll write?'

'Got my word on it.' He pressed her soft cool hand against his lips. It felt good holding her hand and he didn't want to let go. But he knew that no one ever got what they really wanted and at last he released it.

'See you soon, Ellie.'

Emotion choked off her reply.

Through her tears she watched him ride off across the open wasteland. The urge to follow him almost consumed her. But somehow she resisted.

And as Gabriel's diminishing image became blurred in the desert heat waves, she spurred the blue roan into a canter and sadly rode back to Santa Rosa.

We do hope that you have enjoyed reading this large print book.

Did you know that all of our titles are available for purchase?

We publish a wide range of high quality large print books including:
Romances, Mysteries, Classics
General Fiction
Non Fiction and Westerns

Special interest titles available in large print are:
The Little Oxford Dictionary
Music Book, Song Book
Hymn Book, Service Book

Also available from us courtesy of Oxford University Press:
Young Readers' Dictionary
(large print edition)
Young Readers' Thesaurus
(large print edition)

For further information or a free brochure, please contact us at:
Ulverscroft Large Print Books Ltd.,
The Green, Bradgate Road, Anstey,
Leicester, LE7 7FU, England.
Tel: (00 44) **0116 236 4325**
Fax: (00 44) **0116 234 0205**

THE DEVIL'S RIDER

Lance Howard

When vicious outlaw Jeremy Trask escapes the hangman's noose, he rides into Baton Ridge on a mission of revenge and bloodlust. It had been a year since he'd murdered manhunter Jim Darrow's brother in cold blood. Now, along with the sole survivor of the massacre, a young homeless widow named Spring Treller, Darrow vows to hunt down the outlaw — this time to finish him for good. But will he survive the deadly reception the outlaw has waiting?

SHOWDOWN AT PAINTED ROCK

Walt Masterson

When a wagon train is trapped by armed men in Painted Desert, mountain man Obadiah Peabody helps out. He believes they are all just another bunch of pilgrims aiming for California. But among the innocent travellers are the Driscoll brothers — the meanest bunch of owlhoots. Obadiah realises he's got a tiger by the tail when the brothers turn on their rescuer and kidnap his adopted granddaughter. Can Obadiah succeed against seemingly impossible odds? Can he even survive?

MISFIT LIL CLEANS UP

Chap O'Keefe

A senseless killing prevents scout and guide Jackson Farraday from investigating an odd situation in the Black Dog mining settlement. So he tricks Lilian Goodnight into spying at the High Meadows cattle ranch. Lil discovers range boss Liam O'Grady running a haywire outfit, crewed by deep-dyed misfits. She then finds she must rescue an ex-British army officer, Albert Fitzcuthbert, from renegade Indians. And Lil faces ever more problems that only her savvy, daring and guns can settle!